A WISH UPON A STAR

CHRISTMAS STORY

MONTY

authorHOUSE®

AuthorHouse™
1663 Liberty Drive
Bloomington, IN 47403
www.authorhouse.com
Phone: 833-262-8899

Published by AuthorHouse 02/07/2023

ISBN: 979-8-8230-0076-5 (sc)
ISBN: 979-8-8230-0075-8 (e)

Print information available on the last page.

This book is printed on acid-free paper.

Contents

CHAPTER 1

The Unfortunate Incident

This story begins with sad news on one November night as a young woman by the name of Yolonda Williams. Witness an incident that involved an old man being hit by a car while crossing the street. It seems as if the car hit some black ice that cause it to lose control & slam right into the old man. That had a major impact on the old man as Ms. Williams witness how fragile he was? As the old man went up & over the top of the car, while the car slid into a tree with such impact. Yolonda immediately went to check to see if everyone who was involved in the incident was, okay? It seems as if the people in the car was alright? However, the same couldn't be said about the old man! Who seems to be in bad shape, as a concern look came over the faces of the couple that was in the car? Who seem worried about what just happened? Yolonda then begins to take control of the situation by trying to prevail a cool head through it all? As she tries talking to the couple to make the situation less stressful for them? While, also trying to keep the old man calm, so that she can perform PCR on him until the paramedics gets there? She tries so hard to save the old man's life in time for the ambulance to arrive on scene. However, it was a little too late as the old man last dying words was for Yolonda to tell his daughter that he is sorry for everything? As the old man mentions to her that he promises his daughter that she was going to have a wonderful Christmas this year. That it was his worn duty to look after her as her guardian. That with his dying wishes he ask Yolonda for a favor to give his daughter one of the brightest & best Christmas his daughter could ask for? Yolonda then told the old man that it's nearly impossible for her to know who his daughter is? That she isn't sure that she can fulfill his promise to her. However, just before taking his last breath he told her that all the information she needed was in his wallet. Then just like that the old man had succumb to his fate. As she began to cry out for help, while holding the old man's lifeless body in her arms. As it turns out that the old man's name was Girard Nelson & that his daughter's name was Melissa Nelson? Who was living with a friend at the time of her father's death? Do to the fact that her father was living pillow to post to make ends meet. However, he was just about to start a new job paying good money & was on the way to getting a home for them both? When suddenly? Disaster hits! That literally turn Melissa world upside down. However, it seems as if Melissa was a young adult. Yolonda came to determine while searching her profile on Facebook. However, it would seem as if Yolonda had some problems of her own. Being a single parent of one child & having to work multiple jobs to keep pace with living in an upstream area of New York City. Which is hard for her to maintain this kind of living. Which also makes it hard for her to keep Girard's promise to his daughter. Do to the fact that she is busy trying to keep on a schedule between her job & her young son? That she doesn't have time to dabble in Girard's affairs toward his daughter. That she is on the verge of losing everything she own's? Including the shirt on her back. Due to some finance she seems to have trouble with? It seems as if Yolonda was sort of a downer considering how things are going for her. That she sorts of lost her fate in the lord considering all that she's been through? That luck just isn't in the cards for her these few weeks that has gone by & what's worst about the whole ordeal is that she doesn't believe in herself. Which has always been a deal breaker for her. That she is always doubting herself when it comes to getting the job she wants. Even though, she is qualified for the position she is applying for. However due to some bad experience she had in the past it seems as if luck wasn't on her side. Which has her settling for jobs she doesn't want. That is paying less money than she would prefer. Which is where the other jobs come into play. Which makes it hard for her to spend time with her son & to find time to go after her dream job. All because she is too busy trying to play it safe by not taking a leap of faith on herself. That she is too afraid to take a chance on a gamble which might end up with her getting a raw deal like before. Which is a sacrifice she is not willing to take considering that there is so such at sake. Considering that things are so mess up that she can't even fulfill a promise she made to Girard by delivering the goods to his daughter. That she is putting so much pressure on herself by trying to do too much? Considering that her back is against the wall at this point of not knowing what to do. Now that she lost all but one of her jobs. Which makes it hard for her to maintain the bills which eventually led to Yolonda moving into a motel with her son. On the bright side of it all, is that she has more time to spend with her son. Even though, she didn't know where to go from here. However, things would carry on like this into the month of December. Even though, Yolonda & her son Jamie seem to have an okay Thanksgiving considering that things could of have been better. However, it seems as if the two of them were grateful to have each other at that moment. Meanwhile, on one snowy morning Yolonda ran into a homeless man on the street asking for change. Wearing a Santa Claus outfit that seem dingy looking. While bringing her son Jamie to school that morning. Jamie was surprised to see Santa Claus on the street & went up to him to tell Santa his list of things he would like for Christmas. Jamie's mother tries to explain to him that this is not the real Santa. Although, the homeless man thought differently & told the young man that he is not the real Santa? However, he is one of Santa's helpers looking to take any wishes Jamie may have back to the big man. Which was an ingenious idea Yolonda told the homeless guy. Even though, she thought that it was a bunch of nonsense. Still, she plays along with the homeless guy to make her son happy. Which was a nice thing for the homeless man to do? Considering that he didn't have to do it. Even though, she thought that the homeless guy was putting on a show to hopefully get some money in return. It seems as if his little scheme works as Yolonda gave him some money for being so nice to her son. Although, she has no idea what her son asks the homeless man for. As that part remains a mystery between the homeless man & her son. However, before leaving the homeless man told her that she will be blessed for her kindness. As she replied to the same message to him & told him to take care. Yolonda then when on with her day as a sudden good feeling came over her. That today was like no other day. In fact, today was a good day for her as things begin to look up for her. However, while on her lunchbreak it seems as if Yolonda ran into the homeless man yet again. Only this time Yolonda started a conversation with the homeless guy. The two of them would spark up a good conversation that led to her asking him how he ended up this way. As it turns out that the homeless man's name was Rene Grant & that he was no ordinary man. In fact, he was telling the truth when he said that he was one of Santa's helpers. Which had Yolonda kind of confused about what is going on? Considering that this guy maybe delusional & off his rocker. Which is one way to put it or that she misunderstood what he was trying to say. It would seem as if her ears were not deceiving her as what she heard was real. As she asks Rene to repeat what he had said? Which was the thing she thought she heard from him. Considering that he was serious about what he said about being one of Santa's helpers.

CHAPTER 2

Meeting Melissa

The conversation then took a turn for the worse as Rene tried to explain the situation. However, just as Rene was about to ask Yolonda what she wants for Christmas. In came, a surprise as nonother than Melissa Nelson who came up to talk to Rene. What an unexpected turn of events as the person Yolonda was searching for? Came through in a clutch, which seems like a blessing in disguise. Not realizing that her prays has been answer of finally meeting Girard's daughter. To finally deliver her the message from her father's dying words. Which seem kind of awkward at first considering that Melissa didn't know who she was. Until she explains the whole situation about what took place that night. Melissa was so please to meet the person who try to save her father's life that night. Considering her generosity toward her father means a great deal to her. According to what she has been told by the EMTS who was there. However, there was something she been wanting to ask Yolonda since that night. Which was to see if her father gave her some sort of important item like a bracelet with her name engraved in it. Which didn't come across as something her father did? Not according to Yolonda's recollection of something like that to occurred. Which is something she would have remembered. Which seems very odd according to Melissa who can't seem to locate it any where's. That it wasn't with the rest of his things she recovers that night of his death. That was giving to her by the coroner's office who denied ever seen it. As they figure it must have come off during the accident. As they told her to check with the police who was there to investigate the scene of the crime. Figuring one of them must have come across it. Which was a dead end considering that they too didn't see a bracelet that night. Which leaves only one explanation to see if Yolonda has it with her. Which was another dead end to confiscate her present she made for her father. Which seems like all is lost of hoping to find the thing that means a great deal to her. Which is where Rene budded in by asking Melissa was that her wish of finding her dad's bracelet. Which was so sweet of him to ask, but it seem hopeless at this point. Which was nonsense according to Rene who made it his duty to help Melissa find her father's bracelet before the Christmas holiday. That Rene tries time & time again to stress to Melissa to have a little fate. That things will work themselves out for the better just wait & see. Which Melissa & Yolonda couldn't bring themselves to understand. How in the world could he be so sure things will turn out so gratefully in a time like this? As he reminded them that he was one of Santa's helpers. Which was something he wouldn't let them forget. Which they both raise their arms in the air mumbling the words (of course)? Saying it like his words doesn't matter. Although, they knew he met well which resulted in him getting a few more dollars in his cup for trying to lift the two of them up. With some inspirational thought of mind to brighten up their day by a man who seem so full of life. Considering the predicament, he is in? Which is why they both see the good in him even though, he might be out of his mind at times. Still in all, Melissa & Yolonda still respects him for what he does for people. Rene then receives a hug from Melissa who told him to have a blessed day. As Yolonda seen that Melissa grew quite fine of Mr. Rene. As if the two of them share a special bond with one another. How amazing that must have felt considering that she too begins to feel that way towards him as well. Almost as if Yolonda found a long-lost uncle she never knew existed. Being that they both felt the exact same way about Mr. Rene. However, before leaving to go back to work Yolonda ask Melissa if she could stay in touch with her. Being that she too wants to help Melissa to find her father's bracelet. Not to mention, the promise she made to Girard by making sure his daughter has a wonderful Christmas. Which is something she will try to do? They both then exchanged numbers to keep in touch with one another. Which put a smile on Mr. Rene's face? Although, it was clear as day that Yolonda was unhappy with the way things are going. With the whole job thing which is unsatisfying to say the lease. That she is unsured if she will be able to fulfill Girard's wishes. Not to mention her own problems as well. Which Mr. Rene pick up on as he can tell by her attitude of being so depressed. That it is over clouding her judgement. Considering that she is just not into the Christmas spirit. As Yolonda walk away with disgust of having to go back to a job she hates. Meanwhile, Melissa went back to do her normal thing which is to try make to best of it. Considering that without her father's bracelet, Christmas just wouldn't be the same. Not to mention, that she volunteers at the foster home for misplaced children. Who are hoping to have a Christmas party this year for the first time? It seems as if Melissa gets her good charm from her father who always put those less fortunate before himself. Even though, Girard fell on hard times himself. However, before his untimely death? He promises the children in the foster homes he was going to raise the money for their Christmas party. Which is what Melissa is trying to do. By stepping up to the plate to fulfill her father's promise to the kids at the foster home. Which seems impossible considering that she can't find a company that would partner up with her to raise the funds for the party. Which would mean a lot to the children who have nothing to look forward too. Considering that this Christmas would end up just like the Christmas past. With no presents under the tree nor barely any food to go around for a second helping. That it was Melissa's sworn duty to not let that happened again. That somehow someway she was going to find a company that would partner with her to save Christmas for the children. That she just knew her father would be proud of her. Which was the conversation between Melissa & Yolonda who she called later that night. Being that Yolonda could be someone to confine in. Who would understand her, considering that she too shares the same problems? Of people not understanding them, that for ones they can be heard. The two of them hit it off right away as they stood on the phone for hours getting to know one another. The next day the two of them would meet up at a diner for breakfast. Which was a Saturday morning, which was the day Yolonda & Jamie would have breakfast. Which was their thing they do every Saturday morning. It seems as if Melissa was delighted to meet Yolonda's son Jamie. Who seem very happy to meet her acquaintance? Considering that a friend of his mother is a friend of his? Which is how the two of them operate, sort of a mother & son thing. Which is something Melissa can relate too. As Melissa & her father was the same way. The three of them seem like a family sitting together eating breakfast. After they ate their breakfast, they all went down to the foster home to meet the children. Considering that Jamie would have someone his own age to play with besides the children in his school. Not to mention, that it would also be great for him to see that there are children rocking in the same boat as him. That some of the children's parents are no longer in their kid's life. Which is something Jamie couldn't bring himself to understand, so Melissa & his mother sat down young Jamie to explain the situation so that he could understand. Which made Jamie feel awful for the children & wanted to know how he could help. His mother told him to just have fun & be nice to the children. That Melissa & her are going to handle things from here on end.

CHAPTER 3

The Wish

After hanging out at the foster home Yolonda show Melissa the company she hopes to work for. Not to mention, the fact that this company is a huge manufacturer for the Christmas market. That maybe she can partner with them to help finance the Christmas party for the children. Which seems like a huge task for them both to achieve. Although, it would be great if a miracle could happen. Considering that this company Yolonda speaks so highly of? Is considering to be one of New York's finest finance companies in the country. That it is her dream job to work for this company. Considering that she is already qualify for the job. However, she knows deep down inside that with her luck that won't happen. Melissa on the other hand tries to convince her that it is all in her mind. That she needs to step up & own it. That she will never know whether she can get the job or not. Considering that it won't hurt to give it a try being that what's the worse that could happen. Which sort of lit a fire under her to shoot her shot. With all the confidences in the world Yolonda went inside the building to ask if they were hiring. However, her dreams of being a part of the company was shot down when the clerk told her that the company wasn't taking applications at this time. Which broke her poor heart. Considering that things will never change for her. Yolonda then went back outside to deliver the bad news to Melissa who was standing outside of the building keeping an eye on her son, until she gets back. Which put Yolonda back into a slump figuring that her luck will never change. Melissa then hugs Yolonda to let her know it's alright that maybe it wasn't met to be. That something good is going to come her way soon. Just wait & see Melissa told her? Maybe your right" Yolonda told Melissa", That's when Jamie came along to hug his mother & told her that everything's gone to be okay. As he gave her a little wink. Jamie then told his mother not to worry because Santa's helper was going to make her life a little easier. It seems as if Melissa misunderstood what Jamie was talking about when he mentions Santa's helper. As Yolonda had to remind her about Mr. Rene. In which she totally forgot about him. Melissa & Yolonda then decided to call it a day & return back to their homes. In which Yolonda & her son was going back to the motel, while Melissa went back to her trailer that her friend let her use. That was station on the side of her friend's yard. It didn't matter how hard Yolonda try to suppress how she felt. The look of disappointment came over her, even though, she tries to put on a brave face for her son. So, he won't be worried about her. Which was no big deal considering that Jamie didn't seem all that worry. It seems as if he didn't have a care in the world. Being the typical kid that he is, however, Yolonda still wasn't sure what Mr. Rene told her son. That would make him this happy. Considering that before Jamie met Mr. Rene, he would always seem sad. Either way come Monday morning she is going to get to the bottom of it. Considering that he shouldn't get her son all work up about being something he's not. However, the next day which was Sunday Melissa invited Yolonda & Jamie to her church to attend services. The two of them had a great time praising the lord which was well need. After church, Yolonda spotted Mr. Rene outside of the church. She then went to confront him about putting ideas in her son's head about being Santa's helper. That asking her son what he wants for Christmas is one thing. However, promising that everything is going to be okay is another. Yolonda then ask, Melissa could she keep an eye on her son, while she has a word with Mr. Rene. Jamie wanted to tag on with his mother to talk to Mr. Rene, but his mother told him that she needs to have a private talk with him. That he needs to stay with Melissa until she gets back. Jamie than begins to frown up as his mother walk away. Mr. Rene wish Yolonda good morning as he greeted the people coming from the church. Yolonda on the other hand, ask Mr. Rene could she have a word with him in private. Which Mr. Rene was all too happy to hear what was on her mind? She didn't seem all that upset when she spoke to him? She just wanted to know what his deal is with telling her son that everything is going to be okay with them. That he shouldn't make promises to a little boy like that, he can't deliver on. Mr. Rene just smile & replied to her who said that I couldn't deliver on a promise. That he doesn't make a promise he can't keep. Which was cute she told him; however, she was serious. So, am I, Mr. Rene? Told her? Yolonda then shook her head in disbelief, as she wanted to know what his deal is. Does he need some more money, that he doesn't have to keep up the charade because her son isn't here? However, Mr. Rene tries to convince her that this is no con game. That he is here to help them. That there is not any funny business going on here. That he is willing to giving her three wishes to get her to see the point. Anything her heart desire in getting her to see the truth of the matter. Yolonda seem disinterested in the offer that was made to her & wanted him to just stop filling her son's head with the nonsense. However, Mr. Rene insisted that she make at least one wish considering that she has nothing to lose. That what's the worse that could happen figuring she try everything else. That she might as well take a chance on a wish which may seem helpful to her. That he begs her to give it a try? In which, he finally convinces her to give it a shot considering that if the wish doesn't come true, then he would stop filling her son's head with nonsense, as she puts it. He told her to think of something she wants or need badly. Which hit the nail on the head for Yolonda as she wishes for her dream job at the company, she shown Melissa. Mr. Rene then snap his fingers & said done? However, he gave her a few pointers about what she needs to do to up her chances of getting the job. Things like to be more positive that she can get the job & to smile more, which would help her out a lot. Finally, to try & be more persistent & to not give up so easily. He then told her to hold off on the other two wishes until she is ready. That she got until Christmas eve to give him her other two wishes. Yolonda still wasn't sold on the whole idea as she jokes around & said if she goes to the company tomorrow than she would have the job. Mr. Rene told her without a shot of a doubt she would get the job if she did what he suggested she does for her to be consider for the job. They both then shook hands & made an amends. After Mr. Rene shook Yolonda's hand her whole demeanor change for the better. Feeling that there was something about Mr. Rene she just couldn't put her finger on. That he gave off a certain vibe that he was true to his word. Which was probably what her son felt when Mr. Rene told him that everything is going to be alright. Still, she had her doubts about the whole thing & couldn't wait until tomorrow to see if Mr. Rene was a man of his word. Is he truly Santa's helper who wanted to help them? As the jury is still out on that one? Yolonda then went over to her son & told him that Mr. Rene says hi, to him & Melissa. They then went on with their day as if nothing happened. As the three of them hug out for a while at the park. Then they decided to call it a day as Yolonda & Jamie return to their motel, while

Monty

Melissa went back to her trailer. It seems as if the day couldn't have gone by fast enough for Yolonda as she couldn't sleep a wink. However, once she settles down for night she fell right into a deep sleep. The next day Yolonda felt sort of anxious awaiting to see what her day would look like. While, at the same time feeling delighted to finally see if she can get her dream job at the company she prepare her whole life to get.

CHAPTER 4

The Dream Job

The morning couldn't have gone better for Yolonda as she manages her time wisely. As she prepared for an opportunity of a lifetime. However, on the way to drop her son off to school. She didn't see Mr. Rene at his usual spot like normal, which cause her to think that maybe he was hiding from her considering that he couldn't face her. Since he couldn't deliver on his promise to her. She couldn't believe that he got her all work up for nothing. When the truth of the matter is that he is nothing more than a con artist. Who prey on people's conscience? Which infuriated Yolonda, who have gotten so upset that he would stoop this low for a few bucks. Jamie could tell that his mother was upset & wonder what was wrong. However, Yolonda told him that it was nothing & that he should have a great day at school. That she will talk to him about it later when they get back to the motel. After, Yolonda drops her son off to school, she begins to come to her senses a bit. As she thought to herself that how in the world could she be mad at him, if she hasn't put her foot forward yet to see if it's true. So, she decided to go for it by going down to the company & shoot her shot. Just the way Mr. Rene told her to do? However, once she reaches the door, she couldn't help but to feel nervous about it all. That she has two options to either go inside & claim what's hers or become a victim of her own misfortune. Either way something would have to give whether it's good or bad. However, she begins to debate on whether she should go in or not. As Yolonda tries talking to herself in order to get motivated. When suddenly! a voice asks her was she okay. When Yolonda looks up to see who it was talking to her. She seen that it was none other than Mr. Wallace Reid the head of the company standing right next to her. As she did her research on the company & found out that he was in charge. It seems as if Yolonda was in shock that she couldn't hardly speech. That suddenly, her thoughts became scramble & she didn't know what to say to him. That it all happens so sudden that she didn't have time to prepare. However, the door of opportunity was beginning to slip through her fingers. As Mr. Wallace's begin to walk away by telling her to have a great day. That's when Yolonda took a deep breath in order to gain control of the situation. As she wasn't going to let this opportunity slip through her fingers. However, she regains her composure & went to go speak with Mr. Wallace about the job. Yolonda seem so professionally gifted at her craft that Mr. Wallace invited her up to his office for an interview. Things couldn't have gone so smoothly for her as Mr. Wallace was pleased with everything she said? In fact, Mr. Wallace was so impressed that he offered her a bigger role in the company business by telling her she would oversee the finance department. Which was unexpected for even her which got her thinking about Mr. Rene who told her this would happen. Which seem unrealistic as of how he could have known this would happen. That it is nearly impossible to think that Santa Claus existed yet alone Santa's helper seems farfetched. In the meanwhile, Mr. Wallace told Yolonda to go downstairs to field out an application & that he will be looking forward to working with her & that she can expect a call from him tomorrow on when she can start working. He also told her that she will be making a lot of money if she is as good as she says she is? Which brought a bit of a smile to her face as she tries desperately to hide her emotions. However, once she walks out of the company door & into the street. Yolonda begins to scream as loud as she could filled with all sorts of emotions. That got her all sorts of looks from people who thought that she was having a mental breakdown. Which Yolonda didn't care at all, considering that she is now on cloud nine? Yolonda then went to go look for Mr. Rene to tell him the good news. Only this time, she caught him by the church Melissa took them to the other day. Yolonda couldn't help herself as she ran up to him & gave him a big hug & a kiss on the cheek. He could tell by the way she was behaving that everything had turned out perfectly. As he mentions to her that he wasn't expecting that to happened. Which got her to ask him how did he know? Mr. Rene told her do he needs to reminder her yet again? How this thing works. That it's all about making her dreams come true. That it is truly up to her whether she believes in magic. Which causes Yolonda to shake her head in the process. Agreeing to the fact that he has open her eyes. That she is going to tell her son & Melissa about it. Which is a no factor for Yolonda as Mr. Rene told her that she mustn't make a big deal over it too the others just yet. That she must remain silent for now. That this secret must remain between the two of them. Just as the secret remains with Jamie & himself. In which the two of them made a pact about what was said the day the two of them first met? That soon things will unfold in due time. Yolonda mention to Mr. Rene that she already knows what her son asks for. Which was for her to get a better job. Which turns out to be the wrong answer. As that wasn't part of her son's wish, however he did tell him that everything was going to be okay. Yolonda was so excited that she offered to take Mr. Rene to lunch. That whatever he wants to eat is on her. Mr. Rene then told Yolonda about a place that is suitable for great conversation. A place he loves going to this time of year called The Morning Call. Which is a small diner in the heart of New York City. In which, the food there is to die for he describes to her. Which was the least she could do, considering what he's done for her. They both when down to the diner to have lunch & discuss what's next on her agenda now that her first wish has been granted. Considering that she has two more wishes left that needs to be granted. However, it was important that she give it some thought before deciding. Even though, there were so much she could ask for. In terms of things, she has always wanted to do. Which involves the one wish she desires the most which is for her son Jamie to have wonderful Christmas. Which was her second wish she asks Mr. Rene to grant. He then smile & told her that it's already in progress. Yolonda then admits to him that she was nervous about the job. That she doesn't know whether she can handle the responsibilities of a job of this magnitude. Mr. Rene told Yolonda that she's got this? That all she needs to do is to stay focus that her wish has been granted. Considering that all is well of how she can maintain a certain standard of how she handles pressure. That it is all up to her whether she own's up to her responsibilities. Considering the ball is now in her court now that her first wish has been granted. Considering that now it's up to her to maintain her position. Which was the only advice he could give to her at the time. After lunch, Mr. Rene thank her for a wonderful time & went back to his normal routine. While Yolonda went to go pick up her son Jamie from school. Jamie seen the change in his mother's attitude from this morning. As she seems delighted as if she was floating on air. Yolonda then delivers the good news to her son Jamie about the job she has gotten. Which seems like a blessing in disguise of how badly she wanted that job. That now she can make a better life for the two of them. Which got Jamie so excited to see his mother happy for once. That Mr. Rene told him that everything is going to be okay, as he hugs his mother. She then agrees with him told him that this Christmas is going to be a one to remember. Jamie then smiles & told his mother that he has the same feeling. Now that things are starting to look up for the two of them.

CHAPTER 5

The Gift that Keeps on Giving

Later, that evening when they arrive at the motel Yolonda call her current job to tell them that she quits. That her focus is now on her dream job. That now she's up for a challenge to feel some big shoes in the company's finance department. Yolonda then made a call to her friend Melissa to tell her the good news. Melissa was so excited for Yolonda & reminded her that things come to those who wait. That all she needed to do was to apply herself. Yolonda then mention to Melissa that if things go according to plan than she's in for a big surprise. That just may brighten up her Christmas a bit. Melissa seems excited at that point, figuring that maybe the surprise has something to do with her father's bracelet. However, that wasn't the case? It seems as if the surprise was a little more exciting than that? Melissa was eager to know what the surprise was. However, Yolonda told her in due time she will know what it is. That good things come to those who wait, which was the message Yolonda reference back to Melissa. She then laugh & said Well play before ending the call. However, a few minutes later Yolonda received a call from Mr. Wallace to inform her about when she can start. That it is totally up to her when she can start. Without thinking twice about it. Yolonda told him that tomorrow would be great if it's alright with him. Which seems to be okay with Mr. Wallace who told her that tomorrow morning would be great. Yolonda & her son Jamie then turn in for the night to get a goodnights rest. It seems as if Yolonda have gotten the best sleep she had in days. Considering all the stress she was under of having to worry about how things would turn out. Being that now she could rest easily without any worries she may have on her mind. Yolonda woke up the next morning feel excited about her new job. That she couldn't wait to start her career at the company. Of experiencing new & great things yet to come. Yolonda then got Jamie up & ready for school & off they went to start off their day. However, on their way to begin the day Yolonda & Jamie spotted Mr. Rene greeting the people as usual. Only this time he was handing out candy canes to the people who donated money to him. Which was no surprise to see. Considering that he is one of Santa's helpers who wanted to bring a little holiday cheer to the people. Which seems to be one of his traits in making people feel good. By spreading the holiday cheer by wishing everyone a Merry Christmas. Yolonda & Jamie then went over to say hello to him before heading out. Mr. Rene seem delighted to see them both. As they both seem to be in a good mood for a change which is what the season of giving is all about. As Yolonda was feeling generous by feeling the need to give him some more money. Only this time around Mr. Rene refuse her money & told her that there is no need for him to accept any more money from her. Considering that her generosity has been rewarded. As he gave her a wink & told her to have a wonderful day. While giving Jamie the thumbs up on being a wonderful friend. As Mr. Rene also gave him & his mother a candy cane & wish them both a Merry Christmas. Yolonda & Jamie, both wish him the same. However, when Yolonda drop off Jamie to school. Jamie asks his mother was Mr. Rene really one of Santa's helpers. She then replied by telling him that she suspects so. She then kisses him on the cheek & told him goodbye, as he headed off into the building. Yolonda then starts off on her journey to begin her career at the company. Yolonda couldn't hardly control herself as she walks into the building feeling hopeful about her first day on the job. However, when she reaches Mr. Wallace office, she ran into his secretary who told Yolonda that Mr. Wallace is in a meeting. In which she will be attending momentarily once she gets situated. With the business on how things work in the finance department. That since Mr. Wallace is in a meeting it is her job to show Yolonda the ropes. The building itself seem spectacular as of how all the decorations seem to put things in perspective. Of how everyone seems to be in the Christmas spirit. Which is something Yolonda could get use too? However, while in the process of learning her role in the company's internship. She spots a handsome young fella who caught her eye. As Yolonda ask Kimberly Clark, Mr. Wallace secretary who is the handsome young guy standing by the copy machine. Kimberly then took Yolonda over to introduce her to him & told her that this is the guy she would be working closely with. That it is their job to come up with a solution that would help better their company's business.

Doing the Christmas holiday of obtaining a partnership with a small business that can help with the finance department. Kimberly than introduce the two coworkers as they both seem thrilled to meet one of another. As it turns out that the young man's name was Darius McMichael. Who Yolonda was seriously looking forward to working with? Even though, Darius was a little younger than her. However, he was single & didn't have no children. That he is dedicated to his job & was a god-fearing man who loved Christmas. Who seem very sure of how he carries himself? Of obtaining a certain outlook on how confident of a person he is? Who knows how to charm a woman instantly with his persona? The two of them hit it off pretty good to say that they just met. However, they would have to focus considering that they have a meeting to attend too. That they would have to come up with a solution to the presenters at the meeting about what's the best option for the company's finances. That the best way for them to do that is to see who would partner up with them. Which got Yolonda thinking about the foster home that she has been considering for a while now. Since she got the job, which she brought to Darius attention. Which is a project they can present to Mr. Wallace & his staff at the meeting. About partner up with the foster home to bring Christmas to the children in need. The wonders it could do for the company reputation on how it can benefit the company's finance department. Which seems like a great idea to Darius. As the two of them prepare their assignment to pitch their idea to the staff. The two of them would then participate in the meeting. Sharing their idea with everyone who thought that it was a brilliant idea. Which would bring more attention to the company. As Mr. Wallace wanted to know who idea was it to do this? As Darius appointed that it was all Yolonda's idea. That she is truly a person fit for this position. However, after the meeting was over Mr. Wallace pull Yolonda aside & ask her if she willing to take full control of this project. That he trusts that she would make this deal happen no matter what? That if everything goes smoothly then there would be big Christmas bonus for everyone in the company, including her. That everyone is depending on her success. Which means that she has a tall order to fill. Considering that she is now the face of the company. Yolonda told Mr. Wallace that she is up for the challenge, as she is looking forward to making this deal happen. Mr. Wallace then congratulated her & told her to keep up the good work. That there are big things headed her way if these are the kind of things, he can expect from her. Yolonda seem very excited about her future in the company. As her career

Monty

is finally starting to take off just as she hopes it would. That all she needed was a chance to prove herself worthy. As she was getting all sorts of praise from her coworkers on a job well done. Including her partner Darius McMichael who seem delighted in working with someone of her stature.

CHAPTER 6

A Christmas Miracle

At this point, Yolonda seems on top of the world as she couldn't believe this is happening. All thanks to one person who made this possible who is truly one of Santa' helpers. That person being Mr. Rene who granted her wish by giving her & Jamie a wonderful Christmas present. Considering that this calls for a celebration. Although, she still hasn't broken the news to Melissa who work so hard to make this thing happen for the children at the foster home. That her son Jamie is going to be so proud of her. Come to think about it, Yolonda's second wish is to be fulfill as she will be able give her son. One of the most memorable Christmas of his life. Not mention the promise she made to Girard about giving his daughter a Christmas she wouldn't soon forget. Although, she still doesn't know how Mr. Rene is going to find her father's bracelet. However, with him anything is possible. Considering that he made it his duty to do so. In the Meanwhile, Yolonda & Darius begins on the project by sealing the deal with the foster home to surprise the children with a Christmas party. After, Yolonda got off work she went to go see Mr. Rene about the job. As she told him the good news about how her career is taking off. Yolonda then asks Mr. Rene how she can repay him, he told her to just continue spreading the Christmas Cheer. By blessing others with her jolliness. That the rest will take care of itself, not knowing what he met by that statement. Yolonda asks him what he means by that statement. He just told her to wait & see that the truth of the matter will all fall in place. It's just the matter of when, where, & how it all will make sense in the end. Which seem troubling to Yolonda as she couldn't bring herself of understanding the point he was trying to make with that statement. Although, she knew he met well whatever he was trying to say. Although, Mr.

Rene come off as complex at times, which is not all that unusual. Considering that he is considerably one of Santa's helpers. That they are known for their unusual behavior. Yolonda told him that she couldn't stay long because she must pick up her son from school. Not to mention, the fact that she is now extremely busy working on a project. However, before leaving, Yolonda asks Mr. Rene would he be interested in taking part in a homecoming party she is going to give. When she foreclosure on a new house in a couple of days from now. That he can help with the decorations considering that's what he does. Being one of Santa's helpers. Mr. Rene seem delighted in Yolonda's offer & told her that he would be pleased to lend a hand. To just let him know the time & place & he will be there in an instant. Yolonda then went to pick up her son from school, so that they can pick out a Christmas tree with Melissa for the children in the foster home. Which was a start considering that there is more to come in due time. In which, Yolonda broke the news to both her son & Melissa who seem thrilled that she thought of the children. However, while looking for a perfect tree to get for the children at the foster home. Yolonda had mention Darius to Melissa of how great of a person he is. That he could be the one considering that she feels that the two of them have a connection. Which sounds like she is falling for this guy the way Melissa sees it. As Melissa told her to go shoot her shot & see what happens. That maybe it's written in the stars that the two of them met. Considering that luck may have played a factor in her life, now that things are beginning to unravel for her. That things are starting to fall into place. Which Mr. Rene so happens to mention as well. Which all starting to make sense to Yolonda as she sort of begins to understand him. That he was sent to help her in her time of need. Figuring that maybe there are secret Santa's everywhere's helping people like her or worse so that they can also have a wonderful Christmas. That maybe Mr. Rene made a way for her so that she could do the same for others. Which is why Yolonda thinks that she was put in this predicament so that she can spread the Christmas Cheer. By making someone else's dream come true which would be the children in the foster home. That now she is fully aware of the role she plays in the equation. As Yolonda made it her sworn duty to make this project one for the ages. By making sure the children in the foster home have a wonderful Christmas from then on end. As Yolonda wanted to make this deal with the foster home & her company a permanent one. Which isn't going to be easy as it seems considering that there is so much that must go on to make this work. Being that she is a newcomer & all. Finally, they found the perfect tree for the foster home that the children can decorate together. However, the main problem is getting presents for all the children. Which is where Yolonda's company comes into play by gifting the children with presents for the holidays along with the Christmas party. Yolonda then told Melissa about the house she is looking to get for her & Jamie. Although, she wanted to keep it a secret from Jamie since she wanted to surprise him. Not to mention, her own little chauffeur that the company provide for her. Until she is able get a car of her own. Considering that they had to walk places or take a taxi. Only this time they caught a ride with Melissa who has a car. Who went to pick up a Christmas tree for the children? However, on their way to the foster home to deliver the tree. Jamie thought it would be a great idea if the children at the foster home wrote down what they want for Christmas & have his mother & Melissa drop it off to Mr. Rene. Which seems like a splendid idea Yolonda thought to herself. As she told her son it sounds like a plan to her & Melissa. That she was so proud of her son for taking the time to think about someone else other than himself. Seems as though, she is raising up a fine young man Melissa told Yolonda. However, Yolonda told her son that he would oversee getting everyone's letter. So, that she can give them to Mr. Rene who will do the rest. Even though, it would be her newfound company who would financing it all. That Mr. Rene is just the vessel that is taking part in it all. Although, she didn't tell her son that? Being that she still wants him to believe in Santa Claus. The children at the foster home seem thrilled to finally have a Christmas tree that is worth decorating. Now that they don't have to worry about decorating a Charlie Brown tree which they had for the past couple of years. As Yolonda told the children there that she has a good feeling that this Christmas is going to be a great one for them. That she has spoken with Santa Claus helper who has a direct connection with the big man to promise that they all will have a wonderful Christmas this year. As the children begin asking her about the Christmas party. Yolonda told them all that she can't tell them because it is a surprise. That come Christmas day they all are in for a big surprise. That in the meantime, Yolonda told the children to write down what they want for Christmas so that she could give to Santa Claus helper. As she was referring to herself as Santa Claus helper. Considering that it would be her company that is going to deliver on that promise. Even though, Melissa seems a bit baffle that Yolonda made that sort of promise to the children without knowing what the outcome is going to be.

Monty

That she shouldn't put all her eggs in one basket. That a promise goes a long way with these children. Melissa told Yolonda. As she sworn that everything is going to turn out alright. Considering that her luck is starting to come to terms with how she is blessed with the Christmas spirit. That it is her destiny to fulfill what was giving to her to others. As Melissa told her that she is starting to sound like Mr. Rene.

CHAPTER 7

Preparing for the Holiday's

As Yolonda & Melissa was making preparation for what was needed for the decorations to set up around the building. In came a surprise to visit the children at the foster home. Which was Darius & Mr. Wallace who came to support Yolonda to see if she needs any assistance with the project. Although, Mr. Wallace wanted to see how his investment was going. Even though, he had second thoughts about the whole thing. However, he just knew that Yolonda was going to pull through with the project. That everyone is depending on her to seal the deal. Yolonda seem very surprised to see them show support in her little investment. They even went as far as to purchase some Christmas decorations for the tree. Not to mention, hire some contractors to assist Yolonda with decorating the building. With seems to be in the process of negotiating a deal. Yolonda then introduces Darius & Mr. Wallace to Melissa & her son Jamie. Who seem very excited to meet the people that is going to help bring Christmas to the children? Even though, they didn't stay long because they had other business to attend too. They just wanted to show their face & to let Yolonda know that they are hundred percent behind her. As Mr. Wallace told Yolonda to don't be afraid to let him know what she needs. That he & Darius is there to fulfill whatever she needs for the children. What generous people Melissa told Yolonda, that she can see why Yolonda speaks so highly of the people she works with. That she can see why Yolonda seem so interested in Darius. That he is quite the looker who is also perfect for her. As Melissa told Yolonda that she can see the chemistry between the two of them. As Yolonda just blush & shook her head. Feeling sort of embarrass about the whole situation. However, later that night Yolonda receive a call from Darius who wanted to speak with her about the children. That he enjoys every minute of it, meeting the kids that they are going to help. That it almost feels like a feel-good story that needs to be told. The two of them talk quite a bit before calling it a night. It felt kind of good talking to Darius about life & how things are going. As she felt connected to him on a personal level. Which the two of them share that sort of bondage with one another. Fast forward to the next day. As Yolonda got up to get ready for work, she decided to surprise her son with the car service she receives from the company that arrive to pick up her & Jamie. That she doesn't have to walk him to school anymore. That they both can ride in style from then on end. Although Jamie was looking forward to seeing Mr. Rene this morning. His mother told him that they can see Mr. Rene on the weekends when they go for their walk. However, when Yolonda got to work, she was greeted with a dozen roses that was sent to her office. By whom she thought was from Darius who she seems to have a connection with. It seems as if the roses were from Mr. Rene who sends his love by congratulating her on her newfound journey. That she needs to continue doing her thing. That he is keeping a close eye on the progress she is making. That Santa's helpers always know what is going on with the people they help. As he told her that he will be in touch. As he reminded her that she is two wishes in & one to go. Yolonda seems flatter that Mr. Rene knew what he knew even though, it seems impossible for him to keep taps on her every move. That somehow it all seems ridiculous to even think that Santa Claus exists seem far fetch for even her. As Yolonda begin to think otherwise about the whole Santa's helper ordeal. That maybe Mr. Rene knew Mr. Wallace who put in a good word in for her. Considering how it all went down. With him telling her what she needs to do in order to get the job in the first place. That by some miracle she runs into the owner of the company. Who by chance gave her the opportunity just the way Mr. Rene told her it would, if she applies herself? She shook her head in disbelief as of how she could be so stupid to fall for such a thing. Then from out of no where's appears Mr. Rene who just show up in her office without thinking twice about it. As Yolonda seem surprised by it all of how in the world did, he appear out of no where's. He then told her that seeing is believing. Figuring that maybe she needs a little sneak preview of the Christmas magic. As he told her that the magic is real. As she still was in denial until she turns around to leave the office & found him standing by the doorway. That it seems nearly impossible for him to appear in the doorway when he was just behind her. As Mr. Rene told her do, she believes that he is Santa's helper now. That he has provided proof that Santa Claus does exist. Which blew Yolonda's mind that she is witnessing a miracle right before her eyes. As she is beginning to realize the truth of the matter that Mr. Rene is truly one of Santa's helpers. Mr. Rene then puts up one of his fingers as if saying that she has one more wish left to make. Yolonda then turns around while trying to think what to wish for next. Yolonda then told him that she doesn't know what she going to wish for next. As a voice interrupted her by asking her who was she talking too. Yolonda then turns around & saw Darius standing in the doorway instead of Mr. Rene who suddenly disappeared. Which seem very odd of where did he go? As Yolonda ask Darius did, he see everyone standing in the doorway when he came in? Which seem like an odd question to Darius as he told her that there was no one there. She then asks him did he see someone leave her office. In which case he didn't, as he ask her what she was talking about. That he didn't see anyone in or leaving her office. She then told him to forget about it, that she is just exhausted from last night. Darius ask Yolonda was she okay to work today. She told him that she is fine that they should get started with the project. If they want to see some results from the finance department. The day couldn't have gone better for Yolonda. As she found joy in her new career of benefiting from her success in the company. That things are beginning to look up for her to make a name for herself in the company's trait. While debating what's their next move going forward. Darius couldn't help but to notices the dozens of roses sitting on her desk. He then asks her was there someone special who would send her roses. Yolonda told him that it's from a friend who has help her realize the true meaning of Christmas. As Yolonda show him the letter Mr. Rene wrote to her. Darius seems flatter that Yolonda has really accepted her role in being a leader of the free world. That she is really into the spirit of Christmas. That somehow, she managed to get a secret Santa into the fold. Which is a great idea of having this secret Santa to go down to the foster home to visit the children there. While having the children take a picture on Santa Claus lap & having them tell him what they want for Christmas. Which seems like a splendid idea Yolonda told Darius. Wanting to keep Mr. Rene identity a secret Yolonda told Darius that she would have to check with him first to see if he is available to do it. Darius told her that it would really help the company if he were able to do it. So, on her lunch break Yolonda went to go see Mr. Rene to discuss the matter with him to see if it's okay. Mr. Rene told her that he would be more than happy to do it. That whatever she needs he is there to help. That he knows that this is such a big deal to her to make a name for herself in the company. That he is willing to go the extra mile to make sure she is happy. At that point, Yolonda didn't know what to say. As she wanted to know what she can do to repay him.

CHAPTER 8

The Secret Santa

Yolonda wanted nothing more than to help Mr. Rene spread the Christmas cheer. However, he needed to be honest with her & let her know what he needs for her to do. Figuring that everyone needs help with something, even Santa's little helpers. Mr. Rene then told her that she has help him more than she knows. That by helping her he is helping himself in the process. Figuring that it is his job to look after her up until Christmas eve. Which is how things work in his place of business. Yolonda then understood the nature of his business with her & decided what her next wish should be. Which is for Mr. Rene to receive some sort of reward for a job well done. Which seem all good & dandy except for the fact that a wish can't be granted on the provider. That the wishes are made for her purposes only? That he will be rewarded soon enough if things turn out the way it supposes too. That when she is ready for her final wish to not hesitate to let him know. That she has until Christmas eve to fulfill that wish, that there is no need to rush. That she should take her time & think long & hard about what's truly in her heart. Yolonda couldn't thank him enough for doing this little favor for her. That he is truly the man of the hour. Yolonda then share the good news with Darius who seem delighted that this little project of theirs is finally going to take off. They both then made their way down to the foster home to meet with Melissa to tell her the news about what the plans are for this weekend. Of having a little something for the children to meet Santa Claus & decorate the tree. Which sounds good to Melissa who was all for it, by having Mr. Rene come down dress as Santa Claus to spend the day with the children. Although, they would have to get him some new attire to wear. Instead of wearing that worn out Santa suit he has on all the time. After meeting with Melissa, Yolonda & Darius went back to the office to work on the project for this weekend. After work, Yolonda took Darius to go & meet Mr. Rene who they would be working closely with to get him all square away for this weekend festivities. It seems as if Mr. Rene didn't want to accept any money from them. Due to his policy? However, he mentions that they could distribute money to his charity for the homeless. Which they agree to do? That it is his job to look after the unfortunate as he winks at Yolonda. As Darius wanted to know was its Mr. Rene who sent her those roses this morning. That if it was him who has help her with her career. He told Darius that in a way he is sort of responsible for what has transpired with Yolonda. However, it was all her doing which got her where she is today. That he was nearly a factor in the role he played in her success. That what you see with her is what you get, which is a highly successful woman who knows her worth. That the roses & the letter was nearly a proud moment of what she has accomplished so far. It seems as if Darius couldn't agree more, as he know good & well that he is working with a sophisticated woman. Who is a great teammate & knows how to do her job well? Yolonda kind of played it off, as Mr. Rene seen the chemistry the two of them seem to share. Almost as if the two of them share some sort of bond. By the way they response to one another. However, Mr. Rene didn't want to take up too much of their time. As he had to content with finishing up his business by collecting donations for his charity. On the way to pick up her son Jamie, Yolonda notice that Darius wanted to ask her something important but didn't know how to ask her. So, she told him don't be scared that whatever it is, he needs to come on out & say it. Just as Darius was about to say something. He was interrupted by Jamie who enter the car. Yolonda then try to get him to tell her what was on his mind, but Darius seems to forget what he wanted to say. On the way to drop Yolonda & her son off to the motel Darius ask Yolonda does she have a minute to talk. Yolonda told Jamie to wait for her inside the room, while she has a word with her colleague. It seems as if Darius wanted to congratulate her on helping a generous homeless man dreams come true. By spreading the Christmas cheer to all the little children at the foster home. Which will bring hope to their little lives. Which seems like a good thing she is doing for the community. That she can expect good things to come her way due to her generosity. Yolonda told him that she has already been blessed with gifts. That she got the job of her dreams & that she is about to foreclose on a house for her & Jamie. That she got to meet him which seems like another blessing.

That she got to work with someone that understands her & who is not afraid of taking chances on things that matters in life. Which is something she learn from Mr. Rene, Yolonda then ask Darius was this the conversation he wanted to have earlier. When it suddenly slips his mind, Darius just grin & kind of nod his head. However, before leaving Yolonda invited Darius to her homecoming party she is going to give when she forecloses on the house. In which he gladly accepted the invitation to attend her party. Which is also a surprise for her son as she told Darius to not mention it around him. Which seems like a done deal as Yolonda went to check on Jamie & turn in for the night. While Darius went to go take care of some business for the get together for the children this weekend. Melissa on the other hand went to pick up the Santa Claus suit for Mr. Rene for Saturday's event. That even though, her Christmas wasn't going all that well. Since she still hasn't found her father's bracelet. Melissa knew that she could make a difference in someone else life, that being the children. Which is all that matters at this point of making them happy. Which is something that would make her father proud. Which would make her happy to see the children have a wonderful Christmas which is the only thing that matters to her at this point. In the meanwhile, Mr. Wallace receive another partnership with a more advance company. Who wanted to take them up on an offer to finance a Christmas party between the two companies? So, that they can discuss the matter over a nice big event. Which would bring more attention to the company financially. From different business across the global that would expand his company across the world. However, Mr. Wallace would have to decide on what brand he wants to go with. As he was really leading toward expanding his business. However, he didn't want to disappoint Yolonda & the hard work she put in to try & salvage the company's reputation by doing something noble. So, he decided to give Yolonda a chance to prove herself in the meanwhile. While he embarks on the offered that was made to him. Which is something that doesn't come across everyday of expanding a brand like a company of his stature. Even though, he decided to keep it a secret from Yolonda until he can see what she is made of? If she can pull through for the company, so that they all could have big Christmas bonus. That he is going to wait to see how things is going to play out before deciding. In the meantime, the news broke at the foster home that there is going to be a Secret Santa there granting wishes for all the foster kids. This coming weekend, as all the children seem very excited to tell Santa what they want for Christmas. That its going to have the hold Christmas vibe around the atmosphere. Which would be great for everyone involved in the event. That everyone could benefit from including the children. Everything seems to be going smoothly for this upcoming event this weekend. As the day finally came to witness the Christmas miracle for the children at the foster home. Of finally get to meet Santa who is going to grant their wishes.

CHAPTER 9

The Story of Christmas

On the day of the event, Yolonda & Darius help Melissa with preparing the breakfast of a lifetime for the children. While Jamie helps the staff at the foster home to set the tables to start the day with a nutritious meal. It was a beautiful Saturday morning as the children along with Jamie went to play in the snow before breakfast. After playing in the snow for a couple of hours. The children went to go wash up before eating their breakfast. Everything seems fine & dandy when suddenly in comes walking in was Santa Claus. Which was none other than Mr. Rene who plays the part of a Secret Santa looking to grant all the good boys & girls wishes. However, he would have to get all set up before talking to the children about what they want for Christmas. The deal was for Mr. Rene to gather all the children's wishes & give the list to Yolonda & Darius. So that they could see if they could meet the requirement standards of their clients. Which would be the children of the foster home. After breakfast, Mr. Rene took the children back outside to help them build a snowman. Not to mention have a snowball fight which seems like fun. As Yolonda & the others join in the fray of having the time of their lives. It seems as if the bond between Yolonda & Darius was beginning to get stronger. As the two of them spend a great deal throwing snowballs back & forward with one another. It wasn't until Darius chase down Yolonda with a snowball to hit her with. Which turn into a tussle between them which instantly turn romantic when the two of them gazes into one another eyes. Which spark an instant connect between the two of them? Which almost turn into a kiss when came interrupting the moment was her son Jamie who wanted his mother & Darius to see the snowman Mr. Rene help them build. However, when Yolonda & Darius came to see the snowman. Yolonda could see Mr. Rene & Melissa smiling as if they knew what was going on between the two of them. As Yolonda couldn't help but to blush & put her head down as if she was embarrassed by the hold ordeal. After having a great time outdoors, the time finally came for the children to tell Mr. Rene what they wanted for Christmas. As the children was thrilled to tell Mr. Rene what was on their minds. As the children one by one told Mr. Rene the Secret Santa what they wanted for Christmas. After making the Christmas list for all the children in the foster home. It seems as if he has one more wish to fulfill. Which came from Yolonda who wanted Mr. Rene to grant her third & final wish. As she thought hard & long about this wish. Which is for her to have a long-lasting career at her job. She seems so thrilled to have because of him. That she wants to make it official by making this a career no matter what? As Mr. Rene ask her was, she sure this is what she wanted. She then replied, more than anything in the world. That this is her dream job that nothing else matters at this point. Considering that everything is going perfectly that she couldn't thank him enough for what he did for her & Jamie. Then just like that, Mr. Rene snap his fingers & said done. In the meanwhile, Mr. Rene pointed out the elephant in the room. Which seems to be an obvious connection between her & Darius who seem very in love with one another. Yolonda tries to play it off by denying the fact. Although, she couldn't keep a straight face when she mentions that they are just friends. After all, it was clear as day how the two of them felt about one another. Which something the two of them couldn't hide from him or Melissa who can see right through the nonsense. Yolonda then admits that she has a crush on him & that he is one of the reasons why she wants to stay at the company. Since she got a two for one special of finally getting the job of her dreams. Not to mention, finding the love of her life which seems to be too good to be true. As she wanted to know did, he had anything to do with it. Mr. Rene mention that he may have or may not had something to do with it. That the nature of his business remains somewhat confidential. That something just needs to conceal from the world. It just the matter of how things would play out which seems like a surprise to even him. Considering that life is full of surprises that no one is fully aware of? That he doesn't even know how things are going to turn out. It just the matter of waiting to see what's the big reveal. He then decided to give her a little advice to go over & ask Darius to help with the decoration when she purchases the house. Instead of him, figuring that something good may come from it? That all she needs to do is make a move

& see what happens next? So, Yolonda took Mr. Rene's advice & went to ask Darius would he like to help her & Jamie put up decoration in her new home. He gladly took her up on the offer to do a little remodeling on her new home. That he is sort of an expert on decorating things around the holidays. Which is sort of his specialty considering that he was the one behind the company's beautiful wonderland theme. Which is why the building seems so decorative that attracts so many costumers. As Yolonda seem flatter that it was him who did such a wonderful job on the decorating the building in such high standards. That she would be honor if he did the same for her new home. Meanwhile, Mr. Rene gather the children around in a circle for story time. Where they would be serving cookies & hot chocolate. As it turns out that the story that Mr. Rene would tell was a story like no other. A story about a Christmas tale that defines the true meaning of Santa's helpers. Which to the children seem like a fairy tale, but Yolonda knew better? After Mr. Rene finish the story, they all pitch in to decorate the Christmas tree. Knowing what she knows now Yolonda could imagine how beautiful this place is going to be come Christmas. Since she felt comfortable that Darius knew what he was doing. That if he could do it for the company than just imagine the wonders, he could do for the foster home come Christmas day. The tree, however, was a thing of beauty once they finished. However, the icing on the cake was the finishing touch when Mr. Rene pull out a Christmas angel to put on top of the tree. Saying that it would make a great ornament to the tree. Which will bring about many blessing to all you stand before it. Which seems like a great addition to the Christmas tree everyone thought. In the meantime, the children would go on playing for hours. While Mr. Rene & the other grown-ups discuss what's next on their list to do? They all had a good time discussing matters on life & how good things are going. Meanwhile, it was getting late in the evening & it was time for the children to say goodbye to Santa. As Mr. Rene went back to doing what he does best which is to gather money for the homeless. Meanwhile, Darius finally found the courage to ask Yolonda out on a date. Which was something he was meaning to ask her for some time now. That tonight seem like a perfect time to do it, since they had a great time today. It would seem as if the two of them enjoy one another's company. However, there was one problem that is holding her back from accepting his offer. Which was her son Jamie who she couldn't leave by himself at the motel. Considering he is too young to be left alone, that's when Melissa step in & told Yolonda that she could babysit Jamie until

Monty

she gets back from her date. Yolonda seems skeptical at first, not wanting to be nuisance. Figuring that maybe Melissa has other plans. That the last thing she wants to do is to babysit. Melissa on the other hand insisted that she go have fun for a change.

CHAPTER 10

The Big Surprise

That she doesn't have anything better to do tonight other than watch some tv. That it would be great to have some company for once. Besides, it's the least she can do, considering all the things she has done for her. That she doesn't know there she would be if it wasn't for her. That she is grateful for what she has done & now it's time for her to return a favor. Which seems like a plan to Yolonda who accepted Darius offer? Yolonda then explain the whole ordeal to her son who was thrilled to see his mother happy. She then told him that if he behaves himself than he is in for a big surprise come Monday afternoon. Jamie became anxious as he couldn't bare the thought of his mother withholding a surprise from him. As he tries to get her to give him a couple of hint on what it maybe. She told him that he must wait & find out when the time is right. She then kisses her son on the forehead & told him to be good that she will pick him up later. Then off into the sunset they went to enjoy their evening out. Darius took Yolonda to an exquisite little joint in the city. Where they would discuss further matters on how they could better the company's finances. Of what step they need to take to make the company more advance. As he told her about his little side hustle he is working on. To make ends meet with her project they are working on together. Even though, she oversees it. As he made it clear to her that he is not trying to overstep her in anyway or go over her head. It just something he been working on for quite a while. That it is nothing for her to worry about. Yolonda seem okay with his little thing he has going on, if it doesn't interfere with her work. They then begin to discuss their life to get a better understanding of one another. Over a bottle of champagne as they giggle at one another's life choices. While dining on an exquisite meal they order. After dinner, Darius & Yolonda went for a walk through the park. Which was a beautiful site to see as everything in the park was lit up with Christmas lights. Not to mention, the decoration which was off the chain. The Park also had an ice-skating rink follow by a choir that was nearby singing Christmas carols. Which gather a crowd of people including Yolonda & Darius who took part in the extravaganza. As they were handed candles to hold while singing along with the choir. It was an amazing event to attend as they both was in the Christmas spirit. Although Darius wanted to take Yolonda to go skating. She refused to do so, considering that she doesn't know how to skate. Not to mention, she would love to take her son here to learn how to skate as well. Which seems like no big deal as Darius told her that he can teach them both how to skate on ice. Which seems like another way for him to ask her out again. Only this time, with her son along for the ride. That he would love to get to know her son as well. They wrap up the night by getting a hot cup of Coco while taking a long stroll through the park before calling it a night. When Yolonda got to Melissa's trailer she saw that her son was asleep. So, she decided to let him rest, since Melissa told her that she could stay for the night since it is late. The next day they all got ready to attend Sunday's services as Yolonda invited Darius to come along to be part of the service. After church they was going to surprise Jamie by taking him ice skating for the first time. The church service went as smoothly as usual as their day was just beginning. After church was over, they spotted Mr. Rene in his usual spot by the church. Only this time, he was seen doing another good deed by helping the church people hand out boxes of food to the people who needed it. So, they too could have a wonderful Christmas. They stop by to say hello even though they didn't want to interrupt him, seems as though, he was kind of busy at the time. Yolonda told Jamie that she & Darius has a big surprise for him. As Jamie could have sworn that the surprise was tomorrow afternoon. However, this was another surprise waiting for him. His mother told him. That tomorrow surprise still stands only it's much bigger than the one today. When they arrive at the park Jamie was thrilled to see all the lights & decorations around the trees & light poles in the park. However, nothing would excite him more when his mother shows him the ice-skating rink. Which was the surprise his mother wanted to show him. Jamie seems very excited to go ice skating for the first time in his life. Although Darius admitted that it would be difficult trying to teach them both how the skate. However, it seems as if he had a little help in that department as

Melissa was also a good figure skater. That her dad would take her here every December as a kid growing up to learn figure skating. That the plan was for Melissa to teach Jamie how to skate. While Darius teaches Yolonda how to skate in the meantime. While in the process of learning the art of figure skating there were a few miscues as Yolonda & Jamie took a few bumps & falls. It didn't take that long for Jamie to catch on, while on the other hand it seems as if Yolonda was having a difficult time trying to figure out how not to fall on the slippery ice. Even though, it was all good & fun of trying to learn how to figure skate. It became more of an experience than a lesson. As Jamie & his mother has a lot to learn about ice-skating. In the meantime, they all went to go see the choir after giving up on ice-skating. To get into the Christmas spirit. After venturing through the park, they all went to the toy store to get an idea on what kind of gift to get for Jamie & the children at the foster home. Which reminded Melissa that she needs to start gathering household things for the Christmas party they are going to give for the children. Which seems like a splendid idea to Yolonda as she was also looking for household things to put in their new home. Even though, she didn't let Jamie know that she was doing it. He just thought that his mother was helping with picking out whatever they needed for the party. That he had no idea his mother brought a house for the two of them. Which is going to be a huge surprise to him come tomorrow afternoon. Then just like that the day has come & gone. It appears the day couldn't have gone better for Jamie. However, he was in for a bigger surprise come tomorrow as Yolonda made the necessary arrangements for tomorrow's big reveal. As the nerves begun to take affect emotionally of how things would turn out. It would seem as if Jamie had the day off from school that Monday morning. As his mother made the preparation for this afternoon by planning a car ride to look at houses that was all decked out for Christmas. Which will be on the street of their new house. Which is where she will reveal the big surprise to Jamie. The two of them started of the day by going to the diner for breakfast. Then the plan was to go pick up Melissa so that they could arrange for Darius to meet them there at the house. Jamie became anxious as he couldn't barely control himself. As his patience was beginning to wear thin of tolerating the thought of it all. Considering all the pressure he must have been under of trying to begin to process the urgency of how big this surprise is? That has his mother all worked up for some reason. That he could tell from how his mother was behaving that this was no ordinary surprise. After breakfast, Yolonda & Jamie went to go

Monty

pick up Melissa so that they could go meet Darius at the house. However, they would take a detour around the neighborhood to look at all the beautiful houses before taking Jamie to the house. Jamie was amaze how wonderful the houses in the neighborhood is, as he couldn't hardly control himself.

CHAPTER 11

Setting the Stage

Considering that today couldn't have gone better being that he got a day off from school. Not to mention, the fact that he got to look at some cool houses along the way. As he wonders to himself what else his mother as in store for him. Not knowing that his mother was setting up the stage to slowly ease him to their new home. However, there was one house that caught Jamie's eye. Which was a house that had no decoration on it, that had a sign in the front lawn that said Merry Christmas Jamie written on it. Jamie became ecstatic to see his name on the front lawn of a house. Not realizing that it was his house he was staring at with his name on the sign. His mother decided to go investigate to see what the fuss was all about. Jamie assumes that something was up when he seen Darius standing near the sign. His mother then reveals the surprise to Jamie & told him that this was their little house. Jamie couldn't hardly control his emotions as he started to jump up & down yelling at the top of his lungs. As the day finally came when he can have his own room once again. Yolonda show everyone the inside of the house for the first time. As they all were amaze how beautiful the house was, as it was a three-bedroom house with two bathrooms. It was amazing how well it was detail with how moderate the place was. That by this afternoon the furniture should arrive which would go well with how spectacular it would blend in with the accessories of their new home. It seems that his mother landed another surprise on him. When she asks him would he liked it to help decorate the house with them for Christmas. Jamie seems delighted to help in anyway he can for the holidays. However, when Jamie walks into the living room he seen that there was a Christmas tree standing up by the window. With all the ornaments ready to be hung up on the Christmas tree. While waiting for the furniture to arrive they all got together & decorated the tree. It was a wonderful time spending time with his mother for once. Even if it is for one day. They finish dressing up the tree just in time for when the furniture arrives. It seems as if Mr. Rene arrive just in the nick of time to lend a hand by helping them to get settle in their new home. They spent the whole day decorating & getting settle into their new home. It seems as if Yolonda couldn't thank her friends enough for helping them get settle in. She thanks them by treating them all to dinner at the exquisite restaurant she & Darius went to on their date. Which seems like her go to place to celebrate. Which seems like the perfect place to do such a thing considering that this is what they are known for. They all had such a wonderful time spending time with one another, which seems like family to her & Jamie. That each one of them has play an important part in her life, especially for Mr. Rene who made it all possible. That if it wasn't for him then she doesn't know where she would have ended up. That she knows now exactly how Melissa feels when she told Yolonda that she is grateful for everything she has done. Considering that she was blessed & now she could bless someone else which is how it works to pass on the blessing to others. Which is what Mr. Rene was trying to show her in the first place. That he provided her with the job of her dreams which allow her to have a better life for her & Jamie who seem very happy at this point. Not to mention, allowing her to find the man of her dreams while in the process of fulfilling her wish. That she is grateful for everything he has done for her & that somehow, she is going to repay him for his troubles. In the meantime, Yolonda & Melissa try to figure out how they were going to fulfill their end of the bargain. When it comes to meeting the company's financial margin. Which Darius discuss with them over dinner claiming that they have a deadline they would have to meet. Before the company pulls out of their contract. That the contract is good up until two weeks before Christmas. Considering that they need to get a move on being that they only have three weeks left before the company shuts down their project. That's when Yolonda came up with the idea to have a Christmas musical for the children at the foster home to be involved in. That people will come to see the spectacular play that the children has put on. That they can make their money that way to fulfill their part of the bargain. Which seems like a splendid idea Mr. Rene told Yolonda the fact that it could work in her favor. In which case Melissa & Darius also agrees with her. Not forgetting her son Jamie who want to be in the play as well with the other children. In which case everyone agrees on the subject at hand to display a performance like no other. That they need to start on the project right away if they want to see any results. They all finish their dinner & went their separate ways. Although Yolonda ask Melissa would she like to spend the night at their new house so that they could get started on the project for the children. Which is going to take majority of their time considering that they also must plan the Christmas party as well. Considering that they are willing to put their all into this project so that everyone in involved is satisfy. Melissa & Yolonda spend most of the night figuring out what needs to be done in order to make this thing work. While Darius spoke with Mr. Wallace about the whole ordeal with the Christmas musical. Who request more time to put this thing together with his partner Yolonda? Who seem very involved in what she does? In which, Mr. Wallace agrees for now to let them go on with the project. Although, he was seriously considering the deal with the larger company. Considering that it is a sure thing he told Darius. That he is willing to put the deal on the backburner for now, until he sees some progress with their project. Although they need to be sure that this is a sure thing considering that the company could lose money if thing doesn't turn out right. Darius told Mr. Wallace that he is putting all his fate in Yolonda who seems to have everything in hand. The next day Darius went to Yolonda's house to see how things was going. As it turns out that everything seems to be in order. That they are making progress in turning this event into something spectacular for the family's that shows up to their little performance. That they are currently working on the dialogue for the play. However, they would have to talk to the children first to see if they want to do it. In which, they all went down to the foster home to speak with the children to see if this is something they wanted to do. The children were very excited to take part in a Christmas musical for the first time in their lives. The excitement was through the root as the children couldn't wait to get started. It seems as if Yolonda, Melissa & Darius has their work cut out for them. Of trying to get this thing off the ground before the deadline ends. Which means that they are going to have to put some work in. In order to successfully pull this thing off. Words doesn't begin to describe how stressful it going to be, in order to make this thing work for all parties involved. However, they are willing to give hundred percent to see this deal go through. It seems as if everyone including the children was getting involve in giving their best performance. To show everyone that they too matter. Which puts Yolonda in awkward position considering that she mustn't let the children down. That she must see this thing through no matter what happens. Being that she is putting a lot of pressure on herself to not only make the children happy, but her coworkers happy as well. By not letting the company down when they need her the most. So, she decided that she is going to work herself to the bone if she has too. Although she knows that she is not alone considering that she has two wonderful friends who also has her back. Not to mention a Santa helper who has bless her with three wonderful wishes. Figuring that what can go wrong at a time like this when luck is on her side.

CHAPTER 12

Creating A Purpose

While things were beginning to look up for a fantastic performance by the children. It seems as if everything was going according to plan. As Yolonda & Darius hired some people from the company to help create the stage for the perfect Christmas musical setup. In which, they were delighted to lend a hand. While Melissa & Mr. Rene was the co-writers of the musical who would oversee how the play is to be run. In hopes that it would be a successful one. That the purpose of it all is for everyone to be filled with the Spirit of Christmas. Which is the message that Yolonda wants the world to experience. Based on her life experience of having a little fate when all seems lost. That creating a purpose in life is all a person needs to be reminded that there is always hope. Which is something she learn from Mr. Rene that although things may seem tough at times. There is no need to panic, considering that tough times doesn't last that long. Considering that there is nothing a little Christmas magic can't overcome. If you believe in your heart that change will come, which is the first step in how the magic is performed. That this musical is going to be by far the greatest achievement of her life. That when life gives you lemons, you make lemonade sort of speak. Which is a blessing that she experiences first-hand, in which she will share with the world. By doing this Christmas musical which will be forever near dear to her heart. Considering that she has a gut feeling that this musical is going to be one for the ages. Not to mention, that she has one of Santa's little helpers behind the scenes. Who is full of the Christmas spirit that can also perform miracles? It would seem as if luck were finally on her side for ones. That with the help of her bestie Melissa & her partner Darius. It seems as if nothing could go wrong by the way this is starting to turn out.

Not to mention, the support she has from her son Jamie who thinks the world of his mother at this point. Of how proud he must be of his mother right now? Things begun to go smoothly as Melissa & Mr. Rene prep the children to give the performance of a lifetime. While she & Darius design the whole outlook of how people would perceive how wonderful the setup is on stage & in the background. Which is their job to set the scene to go along with the musical as the play goes along. Everything seems to be going perfectly considering that things are going according to plan. However, there were times when they all would take a break from it all & just have some fun. Which was good for everyone to not overwhelmed themselves with work. Especially, the children who they didn't want to overwork. Being that the grownups wanted to make it fun for them to enjoy doing as well. That taking a little time to spend with the children is much more important than any work is concern. That they too, need sometime to relax & enjoy life as they should. Yolonda, Melissa & Darius decided to take the time out to bring a bit of joy to the children at the foster home. By taking them out for an outing to the park where the children could experience ice skating, while enjoying the wonderful sounds of the choir singing all sorts of Christmas carols nearby. It would be something that the children won't soon forget. As they all just had the time of their lives by having something to look forward too. Beside the fact of being confined within the walls of the foster home. That they can now experience what life is like outside the foster home. Since Mr. Wallace took up the offer to finance Yolonda the funds she needed to make the partnership between the two parties that much sweeter. By allowing Yolonda to take the children out on field trips as part of their deal. Which will bring more revenue to the company financially. As they try to widen their brand across the nation in order to bring in more business to their estate. Which will bring attention to both parties. As it would bring more attention to the children of getting adopted by families. In hopes that one day the children can find a permanent home. Which is the goal the Melissa is trying to set as she tries to fulfill her father's promise to see to it that every child is adopted if possible. That she is going to do everything in her power to see that it happens. However, her priority now is to see to it. That the children have a very happy Merry Christmas. Which is something she is very determined to get done. Which is why she is working that much hard with Yolonda to get this project done on time, so that they all could enjoy the Christmas holidays together. In the meanwhile, Melissa though that it would be a good idea if the children bake cookies for the people that is helping them with their wishes. That being the staff at Yolonda's job who work so hard to make this Christmas by far the best one of all? That the goal is to surprise Yolonda, Darius & the staff, including Mr. Wallace for their support. With all sorts of bake goods as a thank you gift to them to show their appreciation for what they had done so far. It seems as if Yolonda & Darius was so busy with making things perfect for the play. That they didn't even notices what the children was doing in the meantime. It appears her son Jamie was also a part of the plan to surprise his mother. Considering that he wanted to return a favor? As he kept what they were planning hidden from his mother. It seems as if the children let Santa little helper make some special gifts for the employee at the company. So that, they could also have gifts from the children who wanted to say thank you in advance. It was a no brainer that Mr. Rene has an ace up his sleeves when it comes to these sorts of thing. That the plan was to have the everyone at the company to embrace the gifts that is to be a reminder of how fortunate we all are? That there is no greater love than the gift of giving. Which seems to be what Christmas is all about? Which is the thing that is going to enlighten so many of people. Once they receive their gifts from the children at the foster home. Which is why Mr. Rene is one of Santa's helpers to bring joy & prosperity to all? However, the day finally came to surprise Yolonda & the staff with all sorts of gifts that would brighten up their day. To show how grateful they are of having what so many other children in need wishes for? To have the opportunity to have a wonderful Christmas for once. Considerably that they were the lucky one's who got the chance of a lifetime to have a Christmas like no other. Thanks to Melissa & the company who wanted to make a difference. Which is why the children wanted to show their appreciation. Melissa & the children all went down to Yolonda's job to surprise them all by bearing gifts for everyone. What a surprise it was? As Yolonda & the rest of the employee wasn't expecting this to happened? It seems as if everyone was in total shock by the sudden generosity of what the children prepare for them. Bringing all sorts of bake goods with gifts that says a whole lot about who they were as a team of Santa's little helpers. Who wanted to spread the Christmas cheer to others? Even though, they are the one's who has it rough. Which didn't seem to bother them considering that they were children who were fortunate enough to have people like Melissa & Yolonda who made this all possible for them. Even Mr. Wallace seem delighted that the children thought of him. What a greater way to bring in the holidays than with a little Christmas cheer. Which seems to be the thing to lifted everyone's spirit. In order to make their job that much easier to help bring joy too all the little one's who thought of them. Yolonda & Darius were clueless all the while long of what they were planning. Considering that they all did a job well done of keeping it a secret from them.

CHAPTER 13

The Christmas Gift

The surprise that the children wanted Mr. Wallace & the rest of the staff to take notices too. Is the gift that keeps on giving being that what greater way to show their appreciation than to give them all a front row all access invitation to their Christmas play musical. Which will be held at the local theater that has plenty of seats for the people that show up. However, the real challenge is getting the word out to the people about this upcoming play. Which proves challenging enough to pull this thing off? Considering that they must raise enough money before the deadline. If they want to seal the deal with the company, for the children to have their Christmas party. However, for them to do that everyone needs to do his or her part in making this thing happened. Considering that everyone has a role to play in what transpire in these next couple of weeks. However, there is still that chance that Mr. Wallace may take the offer that was given to him by another company. If things don't go according to plan. Considering that plan B seems pretty tempting right about now? However, he didn't want to disappoint the children as they were looking forward to Christmas. However, Mr. Wallace knew that he needed to do what was best for the company no matter the cost. In the meantime, Yolonda & Darius took the children on a tour of the building. Showing them all the beautiful site of how Darius recreated the building so that, it will seem more like a Christmas wonderland. The two of them also took the children behind the scenes to give them a better understanding about what they do. The children seem delighted in what Yolonda & Darius job was. As Jamie got to see what his mother does for a living. Which seems like an awesome job to Jamie & the other children. Who took great pleasure in learning some of the things that Yolonda & Darius do in their field of study? However, the secret was kept hidden from the children about the whole Christmas party that they were planning to give the children on Christmas Day. As the children had no idea what was being done behind the scenes. After the grand tour of the building Melissa decided to call it a day & let Yolonda & the rest of the staff finish their work. For them to continue with helping fulfill the children dreams of having a wonderful Christmas. Now, that they all have gotten the chance to meet each one of them on a personal level. However, in the meantime, Yolonda had some planning to do, considering that she has a homecoming party to plan. That she is going to give at her new house. Considering all the success that was store upon her. That the party was for a few people who played an important role in her life. That being Mr. Rene of course along with her bestie Melissa & Darius. She also invited Mr. Wallace & a few staff members which is to be it. Considering that she doesn't have a whole lot of space in her house to invite everyone. It just was going to be a little gathering for those who meant something to her. After work Yolonda & Darius went to go pick up Jamie from Melissa trailer who was babysitting him until his mother gets off from work. The plan was for Yolonda to start preparing for the party while Melissa goes buy a dress for the party. As the same could be said about Darius who did the same thing. Before heading home Yolonda ask Darius to stop by the area Mr. Rene was standing at? To ask him. Will he be attending tonight's party at her house? It was hard for him to turn her down on her offer, but it seems as if he has other plans. As he mentions to her & Jamie that he has plans to meet with the big man tonight. As he gave them a wink, immediately they both knew what that meant. As Yolonda told him to say no more that she totally understands. However, Darius on the other hand didn't have a clue about what was going on. As he wanted to know what that was all about. Yolonda just told him that Mr. Rene is a very busy man who has a lot of work to do? Which seems very hard for Darius to believe considering that Mr. Rene was homeless. As he couldn't help but to ask Yolonda what kind of business he is in, that would allow him to be homeless. Yolonda just told him that he is in the making the dreams come true foundation. That it is his purpose in life considering how he is always there to help another human being in their time of need. In which Darius respond's was that it contains to her own personal experience with him. Which is why she maintains a certain output on life itself. As she told him that he couldn't be that far from the truth. As she told him to let's say that Mr. Rene change her whole demeanor on how she sees the world as of this moment. That although there are bad things that happened. There are also good in the world that breeds good fortunate to some lucky person. Darius then kind of understood somewhat of what Yolonda spoke off. However, he still didn't understand what she was trying to say. As she told him that it's sort of complicated to explain the situation to him. However, it seems as though, Jamie didn't have a problem explaining the situation. As he flat out & said that Mr. Rene was Santa Claus little helper. Which sort of sounds farfetched coming from a young man who believes in Santa Claus which seems normal. However, he didn't expect Yolonda to believe in it as well. Which seems kind of odd that a grown woman believes in Santa Claus. Although, she told him that seeing is believing that he shouldn't judge a book by its cover" Referring to Mr. Rene"? Still Darius couldn't wrap his head around the fact that Mr. Rene is Santa Claus little helper. Which to Darius seems sort of outrages that Yolonda believes in this sort of thing. However, it suddenly dawned on him that Yolonda was just saying that in order to keep her son on a narrow path. So that, behave himself for the holidays & in return Santa would bring him some presents. Which is how it all goes, as he misread what she was doing. However, Yolonda told him to think whatever he wants. That he is going to believe what he wants anyway? That what she says really doesn't matter. So, they decided to leave it alone & talk about something else. Which is tonight event of celebrating a life's long dream. Of having the life, she always wanted for her & Jamie. Although, she couldn't help but to feel as if this was all a dream. Even though, she knew it wasn't. That she has waited so long for this moment. Which is still hard to believe that this is happening? As Yolonda took a moment to take it all in? Before heading into the grocery store to pick up a few items for tonight's celebration. After leaving the grocery store Darius drop Yolonda & Jamie off to their house. While he goes back to his place to get ready for tonight's event. Yolonda didn't waste no time with getting everything ready for tonight. As she & Jamie prepare the food, they will be serving at tonight's get together. They even had time to sprinted up the place a bit to make it feel a little cozier for their guest. Which left them with one final thing to do, which is to get ready for the party. Their timing was on point as Yolonda & Jamie was all set to entertain their guest. Then as time starts to past the guest begins to show up one by one. As Jamie greeted them all by the door by inviting them to their lovely home. It seems as if everyone was having a lovely time celebrating a life-changing moment for Yolonda. Although, she felt some way, considering that the most important piece in her life's journey was missing. That being Mr. Rene who couldn't be there to help her celebrate this wonderful time in her life. That it was because of him that she made it this far. Being that the real surprise party was for him for making this thing possible.

CHAPTER 14

Bad Timing

That he was the one that change her way of thinking about how to see things in a different light. That this was the only way she can repay him for all that he has done for her & Jamie. That tonight was his night to be consider as someone who made a difference in her life. However, that idea was shot down when he turns down her offer. Which made her feel awful in a sense. Although, she fully understood the nature of his business that he must attend too? That either way she still was going to celebrate him no matter whether he was there or not. Being that the party must go on, as they say? The party seems to be lit as they all had themselves a ball. Having a laugh here & there, while dancing to the Christmas music that was playing in the background. As Yolonda took the time to dance with her son. That is until, Darius decided that he wanted to cut in. To take his mother off his hands since Jamie felt a little embarrass dancing with his mother. It seems as if the two of them begin to slow dance all the way underneath the mistletoe. Where they almost share a kiss, until they were interrupted by prying eyes by Melissa & Jamie who begin teasing them. Which causes them both to laugh out loud as Yolonda put her hands over her eyes. Feeling as though, she is hypnotize by Darius charm. That she almost kisses him right in front of everyone. Which didn't seem like a good idea at the time being that their boss is there along with some of their employees that they work with? Thinking to herself of what they would think about them being together. Of how it would affect their relationship work wise. Considering that things are beginning to move faster than she thought. That they must take it down a notch considering that she doesn't want things to go left if things don't go smoothly with them both. After the party was over everyone return to their homes. Except for Melissa who spent the night at Yolonda's. As they stood up talking the whole night about life & how it's going. As they both share an emotional connection with one another. About their life's experience share by the people they love. As Melissa spoke very highly of her father of what a great person he was? That only she knew what kind of person he was, she too would agree with Melissa. That the little time she spent with him before dying was enough to say the lease. The two of them would share even more stories with one another about their families. About Yolonda & her son Jamie & Melissa & her father. The next day which was a Saturday Yolonda decided to make breakfast for once instead of going to the diner with everyone. As the day was shaping up to be a great one as they prepare the children for the final stretch before headlining what is to be the greatest show on earth. However, Mr. Wallace would receive a call that would change the gameplan that is going to affect the outcome of the entire situation. It seems as if this call would be a game-changer of how things would pan out certain decisions on how the company is to be run. A call that is going to affect the lives of everyone involved in the decision making that is going to change everything. It seems as if Mr. Wallace have gotten a call from a certain company who he was looking forward to doing business with. Who gave Mr. Wallace an ultimatum that he couldn't refuse? Only this time the company suggested that he make choice on whether he wants to do business with them or not. Considering that it is now or never to take them up on the offer they purpose. Which totally caught Mr. Wallace off guard considering that he thought that he had more time to consider their offer. However, that wasn't the case as plans change considering that they needed an answer now. Which put Mr. Wallace in an awkward position. Considering that he had dealings with the foster home. That if he takes the offer then Yolonda would feel betrayed by him. Not to mention the children that is looking forward to having a nice Christmas. Feeling as though, he is being torn between the two business decisions. Although, he knew that he needed to do what was best for his business. Which seems like a tough choice to make? However, it seems as if the business offer stands up until Monday morning. As the company gave him a little time to think about it. Which seems like bad timing just as things was getting ready to unfold on whether Yolonda has the skills to show him that she belongs in this company. Either way Mr. Wallace knew that he needed to make the right decision. No matter what the consequences are? That he must follow his mind & not his heart. Which seems very hard to do when the pressure is on you to make a life-changing decision. In the meantime, Mr. Wallace knew that it would be difficult to make this decision on his own. So, he decided to call someone to help him come up with a decision. Which will make things easier down the line. Meanwhile, Yolonda & Melissa had the children rehearse their lines for the play. So, that everything can be perfect when it comes time to perform on stage. After helping the children perfect their craft. Yolonda tries to get in touch with Darius to see if he wants to hang out for a while. However, it seems as though he was busy doing some else as he wasn't answering her calls. Which seems kind of odd considering that he always answers when she calls him or return her call minutes afterwards? She then begins to worry about him. As this doesn't seems like him to not call her back. So, she decided to go to his house to check on him, while her son is busy rehearsing with the other children at the theater. Come to find out that there was no one home at the time. Which has her now concern about what is going on with him. In which case she tries not to make a big deal over it. Figuring that maybe he's busy doing something important & that he can't answer her right now? Which makes sense considering the business they are in. She also knew that he was extremely busy working on his side business, whatever that is? So, she decided to chat with him later? In the meanwhile, she was going to spend a little time with her son Jamie. Since, she hardly had any alone time with her son. Ever since the job & meeting Darius that she hasn't took time out for him. After their evening out Yolonda took Jamie to go & see Mr. Rene since he misses the party last night. However, they had a little trouble finding him at his usual locations. It appears; he too was missing in action. Figuring that maybe he hasn't made it back yet from seeing Mr. Claus? As Yolonda couldn't help but to think that maybe they seen the last of Santa's little helper. Considering that he did what he needed to do by granting her three wishes. Which seems to be the end of their business sort of speak. However, it would have been nice if he could have told them goodbye, but then again? That's the nature of their business. So, she told Jamie, that Mr. Rene had to return to the North Pole where he is needed? In which case Jamie understood more than his mother gave him credit for? Later, that night, Yolonda tries once again to get in touch with Darius. However, she still wasn't having any success with getting a hold to him. So, she decided that maybe he is still busy with his side hustle. In which case she didn't want to disturb him, so she decided to call it a night. Fast-forward to the next day which seems to be a lovely Sunday morning. Yolonda & Jamie decided to attend Sunday service with Melissa. By going back to a place where it all begins for her. Where it all started by giving thanks to the lord above for everything. That once she started to attend church service. She found that her luck started to change, which seems like no coincidence. Which is where she often sees Mr. Rene hanging around making a difference.

CHAPTER 15

A Raw Deal

Which got her thinking about him as Yolonda begin to wonder will she ever see him again. In which she asks Melissa did she hear from Mr. Rene as of late. Melissa told her that she hasn't seen or heard from him since this past Friday at rehearsal for the children. Which got her wondering was he okay & when will he be back to help prepare the kids for the play. Yolonda told her that he is alright, although he left to take care of some business. That she doesn't know when he will return. Which sort of put a damper on things considering that he won't be around to lift them up with his inspirational words. Which is kind of sad in a way being that he was the life of the party to say the lease. That no matter what your day was like he would find the time to say a few kind words to brighten up your day. In the meantime, Yolonda & Melissa decided that they were going to take the day off to take a break from everything & rest. It seems as if Yolonda wanted to spend a little more time at home with her son before going back to work tomorrow morning. The two of them had quite the fun hanging out with one another. Bonding over playing some games with him & fixing him his favorite meal for dinner. They cap the night off by watching a couple of Christmas movies together, before calling it a night. However, just before hitting the sack Yolonda decided to text message Darius. Seems as though, she hasn't heard from him at all this weekend. Only this time she had gotten a respond back from him. Saying that he is sorry for not returning her call do to the fact that he was busy trying to handle business. With Mr. Wallace about maintaining the company's finances. Which seems to be what his side hustle is? Yolonda message him back by telling him to go finish handling his busy. That she didn't want to take too much of his time. That she just wanted to hear from him to see if he was alright. They both told each other goodnight & that they will see each other tomorrow morning. The next day Yolonda didn't feel like her usual self, instead she felt empowering like she can take on the world. That there was nothing that was going to put a damper in her day. Yolonda seem so excited that she begins to sing out loud embarrassing her son who was video chatting with one of his friends from school. In which case didn't have a care in the world as she pop up in the background in the middle of her son's conversation singing. Embarrassing him even more as he nervously shouted out "mom"? As he tries to block her from his friends seeing her. The day couldn't have gone any better as she drops her son off to rehearsal. While she starts off her day building a brand for the company finance department. However, she was in for a rude awakening as she had to attend a meeting which will shape the company's future. That everything will be riding on this one deal that the company decided to go with. While the meeting was taking place Yolonda could tell that something was different about the whole ordeal. That she starts to notice little things like how Darius wasn't making eye contact with her when he spoke to the group of people attending the meeting. Almost as if he was trying to avoid looking at her. Almost as if he seems nervous about something that he was sort of hesitant to speak. That's when Mr. Wallace step in & begin to speak to the group & told them that the company will be going in another direction. That he will be going into business with another company that will bring in more money to their finance department. Which will also expand their brand across the world, bringing in new clients. Which means more money for everyone? Which seems great & everything but what about the children Yolonda ask Mr. Wallace. He told her that they decided to cancel their deal with the foster home as of today. Meaning that the decision was made by him & Darius who thought that it would be in the best interest of the company. To part ways with the dealings of the foster home. Figuring that it was a long shot for them to fulfill their end of the bargain to seal the deal with the company. That this way is a sure thing. That she must have known that business wasn't picking up with the foster home. Yolonda on the other hand couldn't believe what she was hearing. As they didn't give them a chance to even try to fulfill their end of the bargain. That they just dove right in business with some company that promises to help them. With no guaranteed that it will deliver on that promise. As Mr. Wallace told her that the door swing both ways as he took a chance on her idea. However, the different is that he didn't see her plan through. That just because something sounds good doesn't mean that it is. That he is willing to break the hearts of children for some company that just shows up with a bucket of money & thinks that they can buy any & everything they want. Which doesn't set well with Yolonda as she thought that the whole thing was wrong. At that point, Mr. Wallace was getting tired of Yolonda's back talk & was about to fired her on the spot. Until Darius budded in & try to get her to see the lighter side of it. That he didn't want to see her go, considering that she must think about Jamie & how it would affect him. As he told her that he would hate to see a good employee leave the business. Considering that she has so much potential that together they can make this company even better than before. As Mr. Wallace agrees with Darius & told her that there's a place for her in the company to get a promotion. If she is willing to play ball, that the children will understand. That there is always next year to give the children what they need when she moves up in the company. That by than things would be better, he promises her. Everyone in the meeting seems tense at first, until cool heads prevail & everyone came to an understanding. After the meeting was over Darius decided to go to Yolonda's office to speak with her. However, Yolonda wasn't trying to hear what he has to say. Considering that she trusted him & that he lied to her when he told her that his side hustle wasn't going to interfere with her business. That she doesn't know how she is going to break the news to Melissa & the children. As she promises them that this Christmas was going to be a special one. That she failed to deliver Girard's promise of giving his daughter the Christmas he couldn't give her. That she doesn't know how she is going to face herself after all they have done. Of building the hope of the little one's then shattered their hopes & dreams. Which didn't set well with Yolonda, no matter how Darius tries to spin it. Darius on the other hand told Yolonda to take the day off that he can handle things here in the office. That he is willing to go with her down to the foster home so that they both can deliver the news together. Words doesn't begin to describe how Yolonda is feeling. It appears, that the bottom has drop from under her. All she could do was to head straight for her bed & lay down until Darius goes on his lunch break. So, that she can meet him at the foster home to deliver the bad news. However, when that time came, Yolonda was not prepared to face Melissa with the burton of sad news. Considering that there was no easy way to tell her what's going on. So, she came out with the truth which was a shocker for Melissa. As she figures it to be a joke, until she seen that Yolonda was serious &

not joking around. Which infuriated Melissa as she couldn't believe that what she was hearing from Yolonda. Who swore on her life that the children will have their Christmas party? Yet alone, the Christmas play that she promises they would have.

CHAPTER 16

The Downfall

However, it seems as if her word means nothing to her or the children. That she can't believe a word she says anymore of all the people in the world she would be the last person who she thought would go back on her word. That she thought mighty highly of her. Considering that they were supposed to be friends after all they have done for her. Darius then tries to explain the situation to Melissa. However, she wasn't trying to hear what he has to say. As she told them both that they were made for each other. That she doesn't need him or her to give the children a Christmas party. That she is going to shoulder the load on her own. As she shows them both the door & told them to leave & to take her son with them. That they are no longer welcome to visited with the children. Which seems kind of harsh Yolonda told Melissa. In which Melissa responded by saying that she was better off, before she let some job change who she was? Which hurt her to the core as Yolonda told Melissa to say no more. As she went to go get her son so that they could go home. Jamie tries to get his mother to tell him what was wrong. As he seen the hostility between her & Melissa. However, she told him that she would explain everything to him when they get home. It appears that Yolonda was very upset about what just happened between her & Melissa. That she begins to shut down feeling as though it was all her fault. As Darius tries to reason with her by telling her that she shouldn't blame herself. That he too had a hand in what transpire. Considering that he had a role in the decision making about going with the other company. As he explains to Yolonda that searching for clients was his side hustle. That he didn't mean to step on her toes. As he told her that the company wanted to make the deal right away & didn't want to wait any longer. That there was no way he could have known that the company was going to up the ante by wanting to do business right away. As he thought they would have a little more time with her project. Which is still no excuse Yolonda told Darius out of frustration. Considering that he still doesn't get it. That he doesn't realize what they had done to the children that look up to them as role models. Considering that they have no one other than each other. Who was expecting more from them? As she tries to explain to him that how it would look in the eyes of the children that they had been let down by the people they trusted. That these children aren't your typical kids. That these children require special needs, for them to see that someone out there cares about them. Which hit a nerve with Jamie as he wanted to know what was going on with the children at the foster home. As he begins to understand what was going on. Since there will be no Christmas celebration for the children. As he told them both how could they do such a thing. As he storms out of the car & went into the house. As Yolonda told Darius that their decision even affects her son. Which is something she wasn't going to stand for? That it's enough that Melissa is mad at her, but her son, is a different story. As the guilt trip begins to take effect on them both. Of how they could be so selfish around the holidays when there are children depending on them. Which is something they are going to have to live with considering that there is nothing they can do? That Mr. Wallace has already made his mind up. However, there was something that Yolonda can do. Which seems kind of a long shot. However, she was willing to do anything to make things right again. Darius wanted to know what her plan was. All that she said to him is that he is just going to have to trust her. That she can't explained it to him, since it is sort of confidential. She then asks Darius could he watch Jamie for a few minutes while she goes & make a run some place. In which case he agrees to do so, however he wanted to know where she was going. She just told him that she is going to seek a friend for help. As Darius was confuse as of how a friend could fix this? Yolonda then ran off & told him that she will be back. It seems as if Yolonda went to go seek help from Mr. Rene who she spotted walking down the street in her neighborhood. She went to go see if he can grant her another wish. Even though, she knew that her wishes were all up, however, if she explains what happened than he might feel sorry for her & consider give her a final wish. However, when she reaches the person in the Santa outfit. Yolonda seen that she had gotten a hold to the wrong person. As the person she was looking for was not the person she seeks. Which was Mr. Rene who seem *to disappear without a trace. That all she found was another homeless man wearing a Santa's outfit. Who she thought was Mr. Rene which turn out to be a total lost in her mind of what she was trying to accomplish? As she begins to ask herself "Where in world are you Mr. Rene" being that she needs him? Yolonda then returns to her house to gather her thoughts. While Darius went to go see if he can talk to Mr. Wallace to see if he can get him to change his mind about making the deal with the other company. In the meantime, it seems as if Jamie & his mother wasn't on speaking terms. Although, they still communicate with one another. Yolonda could still see that her son was upset with her for not being understanding to other people needs. Which is something she instilled in him. That how in the world she could raise her son to be one way by telling him one thing, while she does the total opposite. Yolonda then told her son that she was sorry for everything that has happened. Meanwhile, Yolonda would receive a text message from Melissa telling her that she doesn't want to see her ever again. Since she didn't see the disappointment on the children's faces when they were told that they weren't going to have the Christmas play. Do to the fact that it's been cancel. Which add to the stress she was under of having to disappoint the children. Now that their Christmas party has been cancel as well. Yolonda then decided to call Darius to see if Mr. Wallace has changed his mind, but he told her that it's a no go? Darius tries to talk to Yolonda to make her feel better, but nothing he says is going to lighten up her mood. As Yolonda just told him that she not up for talking that she will see him tomorrow. After hanging up with Darius Yolonda begins to cry as if her world is falling apart. As she begins on a downward spiral of realizing that things will never change with her. That every time she takes two steps forward it seems as if she takes four steps back. Which is a no brainer for her so called luck of misfortune. That she must embrace the fact that no matter what she does, things will always turn for the worse. As the negativity begins to take a toll on her mentally. That she doesn't know how she will be able to change things now that Mr. Rene is gone. It wasn't long before Yolonda dripped off to sleep. However, the next day when she awoke from her slumber. Yolonda found herself in a situation where she didn't want to go to work. That for the first time she felt awful about the whole situation of going to a place where she feels uncomfortable. So, she decided to take off for the day to think things over. Not to mention the fact that she has no babysitter to watch her son while she works. In the meantime, Yolonda took Jamie to the playground so that they both could have a piece of mind with all* the stuff that is going on. Although, they still were having problems speaking to one another. However, while at the park Yolonda spotted Mr. Rene who was there handing out presents to the children at the playground. That there was no mistaking that this time it was actual him.

CHAPTER 17

All is Lost

Yolonda made her way over to Mr. Rene to fill him in on what's been going on. Since he been away for some time now. Of how hectic things has been for her. Considering that this wasn't part of the deal. That the wishes she made was to benefit her needs. According to what she has been told by him. Mr. Rene told Yolonda that her wishes was granted according to how well she specifies what she wanted. That he told her to think long & hard about what she wishes for. To give it some thought on the matter. That it is not his fault that her third wish was to maintain her position at the company no matter what the cost is. That no matter what happens she wanted to remain that the company. Which was her dream job according to her wish. That she should be a little more careful what she wishes for. That now she is in the position to give her son a Christmas like no other. Now that she has her dream job. Which pretty sums up everything in one sentence about her life choices. Which got Yolonda to realize that no matter what her wishes were. She still ended up on the losing end of things. That all is lost when it comes to her luck changing for the better. That in the end things just end up the same. Mr. Rene highly disagree with her statement about things not changing. In fact, it was totally up to her whether she accepted the fact that this would be the new norm for her or whether she is willing to do something about it. As Mr. Rene tries to explain to her that the three wishes were just the beginning of things. That now it up to her to maintain what was store upon her. As Yolonda seem trouble by what Mr. Rene was trying to tell her. As she begs him to give her one more wish. He then told her that it's a no can do situation, as he told her that she is just going to have to make the best out of a bad situation. That she must take matters into her own hands & start to have a little fate in herself. That if she doesn't believe in herself, then what good a wish is going to do. If she doesn't see it through, when things begin to get tough. Yolonda then told him that she is willing to do whatever this time around. If she gets one final wish. However, he reminded her that there is no need for a final wish. Do to the fact that she hasn't put in the effort to try & resolve this issue on her own. That if she can resolve this one issue on her own then there might be one final wish, he can grant her. Which seems like a deal to her as she prepared herself for the challenge. Mr. Rene then told her "That's the spirit" as he told her to embrace the Spirit of Christmas. That by doing this, she may be in for a big surprise. It seems as if Mr. Rene always has an answer for everything to make a person feel invigorating. Which makes him by far one of Santa's greatest achievements. As Jamie came over to say hello to his dearest friend & to receive his gift from Mr. Rene who told him that this present from Santa was a special one. That he mustn't open it until Christmas day. Yolonda then told her son Jamie that they had to leave because she has a Christmas party to plan. This made Jamie so happy that he started to jump for joy. Although Yolonda didn't have any idea how she was going to do it but talking with Mr. Wallace was a start. Hoping that she could get him to change his mind would be great. However, not knowing how she is going to do that seems challenging enough. As she doesn't know what she can say that would change his mind. Considering how their conversation went last time. Although, their a good chance if she could get Darius to speak on her behalf along with her. That maybe together they could get him to change his mind. So, Yolonda calls up Darius to fill him in on her plan in hopes that he agrees with her. He told her that it is worth a shot as he told her to give him a few more minutes to prepare himself for the meeting. That she should meet him in the office so that they could come up with a plan. As Yolonda told him to hang tight that she is on her way with Jamie. Which seems like a splendid idea to have her son join in on the conversation. In hopes that it may influences his decision making. As Jamie told his mother that he wanted to help to make a difference. Which seems like a sure thing as Yolonda & Jamie arrive at the office to meet with Darius. The plan was to get Mr. Wallace to see how his decision making is affecting the children who sees him as a role model. That making this sort of decision affect how it portrays what kind of person he is? That somewhere deep down inside lies a man who has a good heart. Now that the plan is in place, it was time to go take a trip to Mr. Wallace office to discuss business. It seems as if Yolonda went into this meeting looking to get her point across by speaking her truth. The same way she did when she applied herself to getting this job. Just like Mr. Rene recommended she do by seeking the attention of herself worth. That she works so hard on this project to let it end like this. That she is going to fight to keep hope alive for the children sake. However, once they reach Mr. Wallace office, they begin to discuss the matter about wanting to keep things the way they are. That going in another direction might not be the best thing for the company. That he might be making a huge mistake by doing this. That just because something sounds good on paper, doesn't mean that it is. That at least he should give it some thought before deciding. That he shouldn't put all his eggs in one basket sort speech. Without considering the thought that maybe he is pass on a huge opportunity by not accepting her offer. That for all he knows, this just maybe the opening he was looking for. However, Mr. Wallace was persistent on taking the offer that was best for the company. Yolonda then ask the question was the offer best for the company or for himself. Which started another argument between the two of them on the subject. As Mr. Wallace took offense to Yolonda's question about whether he is making the best decision for the company. As Mr. Wallace had enough of Yolonda's smart mouth & told her that she is fired. As Yolonda told him that he doesn't have to fired her because she quit. Which all occurred right in front of her son Jamie who try to intervene by wanting to state his fact about what it would mean to him & the children if he stays true to his word. That everyone is depending on him to help them with their Christmas wishes. It seems as if Mr. Wallace wasn't buying Jamie's story. As he wanted to know what kind of person would send their child in to do their bidding. Which seem like the last draw for Yolonda as she couldn't believe what she was hearing. From someone she & the others look up too as a role model. Which seems like a mistake on her part that she took him to be someone she admirers. Darius on the other hand couldn't believe what he was hearing as well. As he was shocked by the comments made by Mr. Wallace. As he too tries to intervene by trying to calm down the situation. However, it was a little too late for that as Yolonda storm out of the room with her son. As she told Darius that he needs to make a choice on where he stands. Considering that money isn't everything when it comes to doing what is right. Which is something she is beginning to understand by not accepting Mr. Wallace offer. Considering that it feels wrong in every way possible. Yolonda then went to go clear her things from her office being that she doesn't work there anymore. As

Monty

Darius tries to convince her not to leave that they can work something out with Mr. Wallace. She told him that he can stay if he wants but she is done with it all. That she had it up to here with all the nonsense. As her final words to him is that she hopes everything turns out great for him.

CHAPTER 18

The Truth Reveal

At this point, Yolonda seem a little overwhelm about everything that has happened. As she couldn't begin to describe how awful things have gotten. Considering one minute she was on top of the world than the next it felt as if the bottom fell from under her. As she begins to wonder was it magic that has been store upon her. That looking at it now makes total sense that luck isn't in the cards for her. Which has her questing whether Mr. Rene was actual Santa's little helper. Considering that this is not how it is supposed to be. That maybe she is looking at this all wrong that maybe she is being tested. No matter what the situation is, it still feels as if life has dealt her a bad hand. That she doesn't know what else she could do to make a difference. That she is all out of ideas considering that she has lost everything. That now she is back to where she has started considering that she doesn't know how she will be able to get by. Being that she doesn't know how she is going to pay the mortgage on her house she just purchased. Considering that she didn't think this thing through as she bit off more than she can chew. As Yolonda begin to wonder what will happen to her & Jamie now that things have become so disheartening for them both. However, on their way home from a disappointing meeting. A voice from behind whisper softly in her ear to not give up hope. However, when Yolonda turn around & seen Mr. Rene standing right behind her. She appeared to be in a foul move & wasn't up for one of his lectures. However, he told her that he is here to state the obvious on what is happening. Meanwhile, Jamie seems excited to see Mr. Rene again & wanted to know if he could help his mother. Mr. Rene told Jamie that he is going to try his best to explain the matter to her. In hopes, that it would bring some sort of explanation about what is happening.

So, that his mother could understand the nature of his business. As Mr. Rene ask Jamie could he have a word with his mother. So, that he can explain to her the truth of the matter. As Yolonda told her son to go into the diner they always go to & wait for her inside. Meanwhile, Yolonda begin to take out all her frustration on Mr. Rene telling him that it is all his fault that she is in this predicament. That wishing for something that doesn't seem to influence her life seems far fetch. Even for his standard as Santa's little helper, although he knew that it would end up this way. However, what Mr. Rene was about to say would change the course of her way of thinking. As he begins by telling her that she shouldn't be so hard on herself. Considering that she should give herself a little more credit for being outstanding as a person. Who made this all possible by doing the unthinkable? That it was her all along who made the way for her success. That he was just a minor factor in the role he played in her success. Considering that it was all her doing that make this possible in the first place. As Yolonda wanted to know what in the world was he talking about? That it was him all along who made her dreams possible with the three wishes. Which seems like a no brainer, as he explains to her that the wishes were just part of the plan. To get her to see the bigger picture that it wasn't the wishes that have gotten her this far. That she is responsible for her own success that his role was to guide her on the right path. That he is none other than her guardian angel who took on the role of Santa's little helper. In order to get her to believe in herself. That in order to do that he relies on the wishes to get her to believe that it was him. When the whole time it was her who actual gotten the job of her dreams. That his job was to get her where she needed to be, no matter what it takes? That by helping her he will receive his wings if everything turns out alright. Considering that it was only a matter of time before he hopes she begins to realize it. That he tries so many times to get her to realize it. Which totally caught Yolonda off guard as she wanted to know did, he knows all the while long this was going to happened. To her surprise he told her that he doesn't know what to expect considering that he is just a pawn in god's plan. That his only objective is to see to it that she is well taking care of? By fulfilling both of their purpose on earth. That everything turns out well for her which is his duty to do so & in return he would be rewarded. As Mr. Rene reminded her that it is up to her to turn things around. That she is in control of her destiny. That it is all up to her whether he gets his wings or not. That he's done all he could do to help her along the way. That now she must shoulder the load on her own. He then told her to trust that everything is going to turn out alright. Just to continue to have fate & believe in herself worth. That her intuition is made to serve her every instinctive on what she can expect to happen in the meantime. That she needs to trust that everything will fall into place when the time is right. That she must continue on the path that he lay out for her to follow. However, before leaving Mr. Rene gave her a Christmas present & told her that when she opens it. She will know what to do with it & what it all means. Which will explain everything of how it all pertains back to her. Since she has help him in more ways than she knows. That the truth shall be known by what lies inside the box. However, he told her to not open it until Christmas. Mr. Rene then told her that he hopes that the present set things straight for her. He then gave her his blessings & told her to tell Jamie to be a good boy & that he will be watching. He then told her to tell him goodbye for now. Then in came interrupting them was Jamie who told his mother that the waitress was waiting for them to order. However, when Yolonda told Jamie that Mr. Rene wanted to tell him goodbye. She turns around to see that he had disappeared from site. As Jamie wanted to know where did Mr. Rene have gone off too? She told him that he had go back to where he come from? Which Jamie replied by saying that he went back to the North Pole? However, Yolonda didn't want to lie to her son. So, she told him that he is somewhere watching them. A place far away from where they are. Jamie then seen the present that his mother was holding & ask was it from Mr. Rene. She replied' by telling him it is indeed from Mr. Rene who told her that this gift is special. That she mustn't open it, until Christmas. Which is the same thing he told Jamie. In the meantime, Yolonda went to go have lunch at the diner. While, taking the time to think things over with her son. That her intuition is telling her to first make amend with Melissa & the children. That she really doesn't need to rely on the company to do what needs to be done. That she can make moves on her own with the help of her son. Who wanted to help his mother in any way possible? That together they can still make this thing happen for the children. Meanwhile, Yolonda receive a call from Darius who was concern about her. As he wanted to know was, she alright, Yolonda told him that she has never felt better. That she is beginning to see things clearly for once. As she told him that she is sorry for coming down so hard on him. By having him choose between her & his job that he excels at. That just because things didn't go well for her at the company. Yolonda expected him to follow along with her. Which is a mistake, of how she can be so selfish. Darius told her that it's okay that he totally understands. That he wanted to apologize to her as well for not standing up for her at the meeting. She then told him to forget about it, that what's done is done. That she needs to find a way to make things right with Melissa & the children. Considering that she is willing to do whatever it takes to bury the hatchet.

CHAPTER 19

One Step at a Time

Considering that she is willing to have a fundraiser to help support the cause for the children. Which Darius was kind of thinking as well? As they both had the same idea which seems kind of odd. As inquiring minds both think alike as they both was on the same page. Although, they would have to be discreet about the whole thing. As Darius explained the situation to her. That their plan could work if they use their own money to help jump start the whole campaign. That the time is now to start campaigning for the children's fundraiser. Before Mr. Wallace seals the deal with the other company, in which it will take place next week at the Christmas party. That they have only one week to raise enough money so that they can meet the deadline to continue what they started. Which seems kind of rough considering that time is at the essence. However, Darius manages to get a few key players at the company to help with the fundraiser. Although, he thought that Melissa maybe helpful in lending a hand. Although, the jury is still out on that situation. As Yolonda didn't think that Melissa wanted to have anything to do with her. Since she is still angry with her. Darius tries to convince her otherwise, but Yolonda insisted that they do this without her help. That maybe it should come as a surprise to her & the children. The plan for the fundraiser for the children is to get the people to invest in the opportunity to see the children live on stage. That the Christmas musical was still the plan to get recognition within the company. As Yolonda & Darius got right to work on campaigning for the funds to give the children their Christmas party. As they begin to hand out flyers to the people around the city the very next day. However, while in the process of handing out flyers. It seems as if Yolonda had run into Melissa who saw her promoting the play. Who seem a bit uneasy to see her knowing how Melissa feels about her? However, word had got around that she lost her job standing up for them. Which says a lot about her as a person who stood in the face of adversity even when her career was on the line. Which makes Yolonda alright in her book. As Yolonda wanted to know who told her that? Melissa told her that a certain someone by the name of Darius told her everything that had happened. Also, the fact that she needed help from a friend who means a lot to her. In which they both share a special hug of forgiveness. Melissa then asks Yolonda how she could help with the fundraiser. Yolonda told her that it would be nice if she & the children can help spread the word around the city about their upcoming live event. By handing out flyers to the people that passes by. It seems as if Melissa was already two steps ahead of her. As Melissa show Yolonda the group of children standing nearby handing out flyers. Which was handed out to them by Darius & some of the staff earlier today. Which came as a total surprise to Yolonda, as she couldn't believe the measures Darius went through to make this thing happen. That he is truly the man for her Melissa joked around with her. That he is truly something considering how wonderful of a person he is. That he is willing to do anything for her. As Yolonda sort of smirk while feeling some sort of way for him. As Melissa could see the chemistry to two of them share with one another. As Melissa begin teasing Yolonda saying that love is in the air. Meanwhile, the word was beginning to get around that there is a charitable event taking place at the theater. That they didn't know anything about that was taking in donations for the children. In the meantime, things couldn't of going better for the children. As the word begins to spread like wildfire about their little Christmas musical. It was getting so much attention that it reaches the office of Mr. Wallace. Who couldn't believe that Darius & Yolonda along with some others went behind his back to do such a thing? Feeling somewhat of betrayal by his employees, even though he admires their hustle. Which calls for some action as he demanded to see the people who is involved in this project without his consent. As he wanted to see the main two people who is responsible for all of this. Which is Yolonda & Darius who were obligated to sabotage his partnership the other company. Who sole purpose is to get him to see that she means business. When it comes to building a brand for the company best interests. When the two of them enter his office. They just knew that he would be upset about how they try to screw him over by doing this. However, on the flip side, he seems delighted that the two of them put in this much effort to show him that despite their disagreements. Yolonda wanted to show him that she means well by delivering the goods to his company. Just as she promises she would. Which seems all good & dandy, however there is still a chance that she won't meet the requirements in time. Before he makes the deal with the other company. However, he is willing to give her a chance to prove herself by telling her that she has until the end of the week to provide what is to be the final report. After that, there will be no going back. In which Yolonda agrees to the offer that has been layout in front of her. That all she was asking him for was a chance to prove herself before deciding. Now that things have been settle between them. They can move forward with their plan to settle this thing once & for all. As Yolonda ask Mr. Wallace will he be attending the Christmas play. So, that he can see for himself what he will be dealing with as a business partner. He told her that he will be there front & center. Which is the plan to get Mr. Wallace to see that it doesn't always have to involve money to get recognize. That sometimes you just need to rely on fate to get what you need. Which is something they hope he gets from watching their play. Meanwhile, Yolonda & Darius wanted to know what made him change his mind on giving her a second chance. He told her that he had gotten a visit from someone name Mr. Rene who says he is a friend of hers. Who taught him the meaning of Christmas & how it would affect the lives of others if he didn't first see what he has in front of him? That money isn't the answer for everything, that sometimes you must rely on fate. Which is something he couldn't understand. Until she utters the same reference which has meaning to it. That made him realize the truth of the matter. Which is that he is making the right decision as far as not coming to a decision yet. Until he sees how this whole thing plays out. Which is something Mr. Rene refer he do, considering what does he have to lose at this point. That if one situation doesn't work out, then he can go with the second choice. Which will be beneficial to him either way he looks at it. Which makes perfect sense to him from a business standard. As Yolonda told Mr. Wallace that Mr. Rene was the reason behind her success. That he is sort of her mentor. Which would explain where she gets all her intelligence from, Mr. Wallace said to her. As she couldn't disagree with that statement. As she pointed out the fact that he is the reason behind the woman she is today. Which is a strong independent woman who values herself worth. Which is something Mr. Wallace can relate too, as a businessman who just loves the way she handles business with such self-confidence. As he can see the influence Mr. Rene had on

Monty

her life, as he did the same for him. It seems to Darius that Mr. Rene is truly someone who has made a difference. Considering that he comes off as a person who couldn't help himself being homeless & all. However, Mr. Wallace would describe Mr. Rene as a well-kept man who values looking like a millionaire who just hit the lotto. Which seem impossible, as Yolonda & Darius wanted to know were they talking about the same person.

CHAPTER 20

The Christmas Resolution

All Mr. Wallace knows is that Mr. Rene told him that his fate lies by the choices he makes. Whether that be good or bad decisions which will resolve any conflict he may have. That he must follow his heart. Which brings Mr. Wallace to the second reason he decided to give Yolonda a second chance to prove herself worthy. As he begins to tell the story about the times he was coming up as a child. As he begins telling Yolonda & Darius that he grew up poor & that his mother was a single parent who raise him the best way she could. That there were many times they would sleep in shelters around town. However, his mother was determined to teach him how to survive the hardship of reality. By teaching him the basic form of education, so that one day he can grow up to be someone special. That her one rule to the game is to look out for number one. Which is him to do whatever he needed to in order to survive this harsh reality. That her teaching has made him the person he is today. Which is why he is the way that he is? Until Mr. Rene came along & change his thought process. As he had to look himself in the mirror, for him to realize where he had come from. That some where's deep inside lies that young boy who came from nothing. Who needed help, for him to become the man he is today? Which may have come at a price if he didn't have someone to like his mother to look up too. Which is how the children must feel, since they have no one to look up too. Who can teach them the same way his mother did for him? Not to mention a role model that they can look up too. Who cares about their well-being, which put things into prospective on how he presents himself? Considering that the children are paying close attention to what he does. The same way he did with his mother. Which is why he decided to give it another shot to see if a deal can

*be made with the foster home before the deadline. Which inspire Yolonda &
Darius to make this deal happened no matter what the consequences are. As
Mr. Wallace told them both to go out & make him proud. As they both set out
to seal the deal between the two parties. However, before leaving Mr. Wallace
office. Yolonda told him that his mother would be proud of him. For what he
is doing for others who were just like him. Considering that he has help her
along the way & that it is her job to do the same for the children. That he has
provide her the opportunity of a lifetime. By giving her a chance to redeem
herself reliance to the company. That she is willing to give it everything she
got to make this thing happened. Considering that everything is on the line as
of how this thing would turn out. That if it doesn't go well then, she can say
that she has done her best. Time was at the essence of filling the theater seats
for the musical. As they race against time to hand out as many flyers, they
could to anyone who were interested in going. As the money for the fundraiser
for the play was beginning to skyrocket beyond what they expected. Although,
they didn't know how much they would take in, until the play was over. That
way they can gather up all the money they collect to see if it is enough to make
the deal official. As the days begin to pass things begin to look up for their
expectation. Then the day finally came to do the Christmas musical. As they
all were expecting a full house for tonight's big event. At that point, the nerves
begin to settle in, as the time begins to draw near. As the children prepare
one final time to remember their lines for the play. It seems as if the people
who is involved in this event show up & show out for this once & a lifetime
occasion. As the crowd begin to pour in the theater to see this great play that
the children as put on for them. Make or break, this performance is going to
be none like no other. As the children prepare to take their place on stage to
give the people what they want. Which is to give the people their money worth.
By performing greatly on stage to perfection. By owning their craft to connect
with the audience with their performance. Which is easy said than done, as
the children went out & accomplish what they set out to do? Which is to wow
the audience & own the stage with their performance. As the children receive
a standing ovation at the end of the musical. Which was a feel-good moment
for them all. That for once in their little lives they felt that people finally begin
to see them for who they are. Which is what Melissa & the others was trying to
achieve. By shining a spotlight on foster care for the children. Who is looking to
get adopted by a loving family. It seems as if Yolonda & the others couldn't be*

prouder of them for doing a great job. However, in the distance Yolonda could have sworn she seen Mr. Rene giving her a round of applause for a job well done. Although, it appears as if she was the only one who can see him. Do to the fact that everyone in the crowd who was leaving didn't notice him. However, when she tries to get his attention by going up to meet him. He suddenly vanished into thin air without a trace of his whereabouts. In the meantime, Yolonda had some business to attend too. As her focus shifted to see if they gather enough money to seal the deal with the company. On the other end Mr. Wallace was pleased with the children's performance. As it touches his heart with such emotions of what it means to have The Spirit of Christmas inside of you. Which touch a lot of people who experience it firsthand coming from a group of foster kids. Who set an example for those who are fortunate enough to have witness this miracle of a performance in the eyes of children? Who seem to have all the answers for life's experience of what it means to be given a chance? That this is the time of the season for giving. Which was the whole demeanor behind the musical to get people into the holiday spirit. Which was the vision Yolonda had when she thought about this musical. Which turn out better than she expected it would. However, things would turn for the worse as Yolonda & the others discover that they came up just a little bit short of the money needed to seal the deal. Which put a damper on everyone's spirit that they were so close in making this deal happened. That even with charity that was raise for the children wasn't enough. Figuring that she now must take the lost. That she did her best Darius told her as Yolonda begins to cry. Although, her son Jamie & Melissa along with the children didn't want to blame her for what happened. They told her that it's just the way things are for them. In which she could understand considering the bad luck she had to endure. Which is something Yolonda couldn't bring herself to understand. Of what's the purpose for her to bring joy to others, if she can't even fulfill a simple promise to live up her end of the bargain. Which seems unfortunate at the time of why this is happening. As she told Melissa that she fail her & the children. That she swore that the children would have a Christmas party. Not to mention, the promise Yolonda made to her father about giving her a wonderful Christmas. Which is something Yolonda kept from Melissa considering that she didn't want to tell her & not be able to deliver on the promise. Which was his last words to her? Yolonda explains to Melissa, as she told her everything that went on between her & Melissa's father. As Yolonda show Melissa a picture her father gave her from his wallet along with her name. Which would explain how Yolonda was able to find her. Which would also explain why she wanted to befriend her as well. Which was a bit much for Melissa who seem very emotional at the time of hearing all this for the first time. Which would explain everything that has gone on.

CHAPTER 21

The Spirit of Christmas

Melissa seems very grateful that Yolonda would go through all of this for her father's promise to her. Which seem kind of notable of her to do. As Melissa gave her a great big hug & told her that she is sorry for the way she behaves toward her about the children. Yolonda told her that it was okay that she knows that she didn't really mean it. Melissa then told Yolonda that she is grateful for what she tries to do for her & the children. Although, it didn't go the way she planned, it was the thought that counted. As Melissa told Yolonda not to get upset that they are going to figure something out to do for the children on Christmas day. That having the Christmas play was one good thing they did for the children. Considering that now they brought some attention to the foster home. That people are willing to consider adopting them. Which is good enough for her as a Christmas wish. Which kind of easy Yolonda's pain a bit of knowing that she done some good for the children? That no one was upset nor mad at her for trying to do her best. Which sort of put things into prospective of not being too hard on herself when something doesn't go right. Considering that she has done better than she knows. Which is why she receive an around of applause from not only Mr. Rene, but the entire crowd who thought she done great. Not to mention her son Jamie who couldn't be prouder of his mother for what she has accomplish. That for once she could understand that it's not about the presents, but the gift of giving which is all that matters. In which case she gave the children what they needed which is to shine a light on their situation. Which is the best present anyone of them could receive. Which is also a gift for Melissa who wouldn't wanted any other way. Come Monday morning Yolonda would receive great news from her job. As she walks into her office to find out that they have an important meeting to attend too. Containing to the new company her boss is doing business with. Which seem all too familiar of why this person call in a meeting now. When the discussion about the deal was supposed to be over the holidays at the Christmas party. Which has everyone puzzle at this point of what the big idea for this meeting. That had some people afraid of what this might mean for the company. Figuring that maybe the company may go in a different direction for all they know. Which may cost some of them their jobs considering the type of deal that was made. Knowing that this person behind the scenes has a reputation for changing things up a bit. To make the company better according to Mr. Wallace who needed some changes done. In order to expand his business franchise so that the company could reach multiple clients in the industry. Rumors begin to circulate that not even Mr. Wallace knew what the meeting was about. Which was a chance he was willing to take to see what kind of offer this person is willing to make on his behalf. Which has everyone nervous of what direction this person is going to take. As the meeting begun to get started it turns out that things weren't as bad as it seems. That the person seems cool headed about negotiating a deal that would pique everyone interest. Considering that there has been a change of plans for the Christmas party. Considering that this person & his partners are seriously reconsidering giving back to the community. By hosting a Christmas party for the children at the foster home. That they are willing to put up the rest of the money needed to make this deal happened. Although, this deal will be part of the partnership of a third party. As this person along with his partners wanted in on the deal. Considering that this offer is by far one of the most decorated decision-making proposals ever made by a company. To go in the direction, they did. Which was smart on their part of going into business with a corporation that must deal with foster children to build up their company's brand. As this person wanted to know who idea it was to do this deal. Which had everyone in the room turn toward Yolonda. As Mr. Wallace told the guy that it was all her idea. Which had the guy impress with Yolonda & how she come off as a professional when it comes to her job. As Mr. Wallace spoke very highly of her which is the reason, he has hired her in the first place. That she has the potential to move up to in the ranking. Meaning that she has been promoted up to senior executive of the company along with Darius. As they both seem shocked by the sudden news that they have move up in the company. Especially, Yolonda who move up so quickly, which means more pay for her & the other employees who will receive a Christmas bonus. However, there was one thing Mr. Wallace & the others wanted to know about. Is how they knew about the deal with the foster home which seem simple enough? As the guy begin to explain that they do their homework on companies they attend to do business with & found out that way. Plus, he & a couple of his partners attended the Christmas play & love it. Which made the decision that much easier? It seems as if things were finally starting to unfold just the way Mr. Rene said it would. That all she needed to do is to be patient & things will begin to unravel. Considering that things are going to work themselves out for the better. However, Yolonda couldn't wait to deliver the good news to Melissa who was babysitting her son at the foster home helping the children. Prepare for what seems like another lost Christmas. However, that would all change when the contractors showed up to deliver the goods to the children. By turning the foster home into a Christmas wonderland in under a week, just in time for Christmas. As the children was surprise Christmas morning when they awoke to find presents under the tree for them. Which was a very exciting thing to see the children happy. That they finally get the Christmas they deserve. As Yolonda, Melissa & Darius watch from a distance while Jamie & the others open their gifts. As they all got up early Christmas morning so that they could be there when the children wake up. As Jamie wanted to open his gifts along with the children, as he told his mother to bring his presents to the foster home. So, that he can share this experience with the children. It seems as if Yolonda, Melissa & Darius all gotten gifts for one another. As they join in on the party of seeing what gifts they receive from each other along with a special gift that the children got for them. Which was the gift of appreciation for all of what they had done for them. By giving them all a medal made especially for the three of them. Which says a lot about how grateful they are to have people like them. Who made their day by giving them a Christmas they won't never forget? However, Yolonda told the children to get used to it, because they can expect this to happen every year from then on end. That a deal has been made to make it official for the children that is here & for the children that comes after them. Until they can find a family to adopt them. Which is some else that is in progress in hopes that will happen soon. Meanwhile, Yolonda went some place alone to open the gift she receives from Mr. Rene who told her that the gift was a special one. Which would explain everything. However, when she opens the gift, she seen a note on the side of a bracelet that had Melissa name carved in it. At that point, Yolonda realize that Mr. Rene has found her father's bracelet. Although, the note was written to her, as Yolonda begins to read the note that says. That he is grateful that she was able to fulfill his promise to his daughter. That she has help him more ways than she knows. Which is why he decided to return a favor. It was then, that Yolonda realize that her guardian angel was none other than the man she tries to save on that fateful night of the accident. Which was Melissa's father Girard who came back in a different form because of his unfinished business. He had promised his daughter while being in transition of becoming an angel by helping her in the process of repaying his depth to her for trying to save him. Which is a process of turning the corner when it comes to redefining the circle of life. That she can expect good things when she tries to do good in the world. This unexpected turn of event sort of uncommon to say the least. As Yolonda wasn't expecting that to occur, as she has gotten the surprise of lifetime. Although, he told her to promise him not to say a word about it to anyone. That this conversation should stay between the two of them. So, Yolonda tore up the note & threw it in the fireplace. However, she reunited her father's bracelet with its rightful owner. Which was Melissa who was elated that Yolonda found her father's bracelet. Even though, it wasn't her she told Melissa. That it was Mr. Rene who recover her father's bracelet just as he promises. As Melissa told Yolonda that Mr. Rene was indeed Santa's little helper. As Yolonda couldn't agree more with her. As she told Melissa that Mr. Rene is more like a little angel who is watching over them. As Melissa totally agrees with her by saying who would think that he is one of a kind. Not knowing the extent of his true purpose which will remain hinted from her. As the time finally came to surprise the children with their very own Christmas party. In which everyone from the two companies attended making everyone's holiday a one to remember. As Jamie showed his mother the gift that Mr. Rene got for him. Which was a pair of ice skates for when he goes ice skating again with his mother & Darius. However, nothing would make a happy ending then sealing it with a kiss underneath the mistletoe share by Yolonda & her newfound boyfriend Darius. Who seem to make it official by showing their true feeling for one another?

The End

Printed in the United States
by Baker & Taylor Publisher Services